I0670868

Shallow Water

Intrigue

A Story of Romance and Mystery

by

Anna Leigh

A Sandy Bay Romance

Dedication

To You.
Yes. You.

ACKNOWLEDGMENTS

No book can be completed without the help of many others, usually too numerous to mention all by name. Here are a few, and forgive me if I have excluded anyone – I would write anyone important, but you are all important to me.

First, my family without who's encouragement this would have not been completed. Especially my mom, who always believed. Then, to the group of reviewers who provide valuable insight and impetus for changing this work in ways to make it better, **especially Laura and Elena,** and to all those others for helping me to accomplish my goals – my readers who have made this effort a joy.

Finally, my gratitude and debt to the editor of this work, Jessica Snyder (jessicasnyderedits@gmail.com) who not only offered great insights and ideas to make this a better work, but also provided encouragement and praise.

Cover by

Evocative X

99 designs

The purpose of life is to live.

Look around you now
You must go for what you wanted
Look at all my friends who did
And got what they deserved.

Wasted on the Way – Crosby, Stills, & Nash

For small creatures such as we, the vastness is bearable only through love.
Carl Sagan

People sleep peaceably in their beds at night only because men and women stand ready to do violence on their behalf.
A la George Orwell

You play stupid games; you win stupid prizes.
Unknown

One

First Class Petty Officer Kristi Swanson's arms ached as she gripped the helm. Her strength was all but drained from her body. Waves, driven by strong, gusting winds, slapped the sides of the small rescue boat, throwing it wildly. Her compass swung erratically. Steering the boat and reading any of the instruments were almost impossible. She didn't have to look at the gauge to know her fuel was dangerously low. She squinted into the blackness of the night beyond the windscreen as raindrops smashed against it. More than anything, she wanted to be back at base, warm, dry, and safe. Not out here – cold, wet, and at the mercy of the ocean and storm.

Three people huddled behind her – a man, his wife, and their six-year-old daughter. She didn't want them to know they were in danger, and she was scared. She didn't want to come out here alone, but she'd had no choice. Unless she'd decided to let these people die.

She pressed the button on the microphone, "Coast Guard Base Sandy Bay, this is rescue nine-five alpha," her voice breaking as the boat smashed into a wave. There was no response. She repeated the call. It seemed like forever before she heard, "Nine five alpha, Sandy Bay."

She sighed, and a wave of relief washed over her. "Sandy Bay, nine-five alpha. Inbound with three from the Francine. They seem to be okay. Have McPherson meet us to give them a quick check before we send them to the clinic."

"Understood. ETA?"

"About twenty-five minutes, if my fuel holds out," she said, with a glance at the slim margin between the needle and the black "E" on the gauge as a large wave washed over the boat, rolling it. She tilted her head to the side to make the needle appear farther off the empty line than it was. "Should be okay." She hoped.

"Understood. Let us know if anything changes."

"Stand by to meet us. I'll want some help with our passengers."

She turned and looked at the passengers. Somber faces, except for the girl who seemed to be enjoying this unexpected ride. When Kristi had reached their sinking boat, the brown-haired girl, Amber, with big eyes, had said, "Are you really in the Coast Guard?" She smiled.

"So, Mister Johnson, tell me again what happened," she said over her shoulder to the man huddled in the seat behind her.

"Uh, not much to tell. We were headed up the coast. We hit something in the water. I thought it might be a whale. Maybe something else. I don't know. I never saw it – before or after. Must have cracked my hull. We started to take on water.

2

Smashed the prop, too, I think. Didn't take long to figure out we were in trouble. That's when I called. Thank God you got there when you did. I don't think we'd stay afloat much longer." He hugged his wife and kissed his daughter on the top of her head.

Kristi shuddered. She didn't want to picture what would have happened if she hadn't gotten to them in time. She looked up and saw the station lights on the horizon through a momentary parting in the curtain of rain. She sighed, rolled her eyes to heaven, and said a short prayer of thanks.

Twenty-two minutes later, the response boat entered the small inlet. Sheltered from the worst of the storm, the sea was calmer. She steered toward the pier and two men standing on it. Pritchett and McPherson.

The boat bumped softly, and both men threw lines to tie up the bow and stern. Then, they helped the Johnsons out of the craft and onto land. A light rain was falling.

"Petty officer McPherson is our medical technician. He's going to do a quick check before we get you to the clinic for a more comprehensive exam. He'll take good care of you," she said with a smile.

"Pritchett," she said, turning to the other man, "better fill her up. We may need to go back out. Oh, and could you microwave some broth or tea or something for them to drink. They've got to be freezing."

Pritchett acknowledged with a nod, then said, "You really want to go back out?"

"No. One trip tonight was enough for me, but we're not the ones who say when we go. Semper Paratus, remember?" She said it with more conviction than she felt.

She turned and walked toward a large red-brick building on leaden legs. It was an old seaplane hangar that had been converted into their station. The seaplanes had been gone for years. She entered the women's locker room and headed for her locker. She striped off her wet clothes, shivering as the cold night air hit the moisture on her skin. *Should have turned on the shower first*, she thought.

She grabbed a towel, wrapped it around herself, and headed to the shower. She turned on the tap, impatient for the water to heat. In less than a minute, the shower was steaming. She stepped in and shivered again as the first of the water spray hit the front of her body. She turned a knob, and hot water washed over her from above and from the front. It was a gift to the station from a former senior petty officer. It sprayed water from two directions at once.

The hot water ran over her head, shoulders, and down her body. It was heavenly, and she closed her eyes, luxuriating in one of life's pleasures. *Nothing better than a hot shower when you need one*. The water caused her to relax, and the adrenalin of the rescue was wearing off. She was shaking slightly, and fatigue was hitting her hard. She hoped there wouldn't be another rescue tonight. She didn't have the strength. Maybe McPherson and Pritchett could make any additional runs. She felt lucky to have completed that one by herself.

Slowly, she washed her hair, then soaped up and rinsed off. Clean, relaxed, and refreshed, she turned off the shower and stepped back into the locker room. She dried herself and put on a clean work uniform. She dried her dark blond hair and put it into a ponytail. It was long for service regs, and during the day, or around seniors, she French-braided it and wore it up.

She took a deep breath, left the locker room, and headed to the small sick bay.

"They're all fine," said McPherson, anticipating her question. "Cold from the ordeal and a little shaken. We've arranged transport. Should be here in about ten minutes."

"Good."

"The husband, uh father, is really upset. I mean, really. I thought about giving him a sedative."

"Yeah, well, he's the captain. He decided to go out, and that decision almost got them all killed," she said.

Mr. Johnson stood and walked over to them. "I – I want to thank you. I could have. I mean, I knew there might be a storm, but I didn't think it would be that bad. I could have," he let the thought die out.

"Well, sir, I'm glad it worked out the way it did. You lost your boat, but your family is safe. I assume the boat was insured."

"Huh? Yes. Of course. Insured." His eyes met hers, then darted to the floor. "I just – thank you. Thank you so very much." Then, he turned and walked back to his family.

"I see what you mean. Anyway, write up your findings and slip them into my inbox. I'll write the report in the morning." She yawned. "God, I hope I don't have to go out again tonight. I'm shot. And, come to think of it, starved."

"I ordered pizza for dinner. Some left in the fridge. Help yourself."

"Thanks. No fish?" she asked.

"No. No fish. I don't do fish on my pizza. Anyway, it's Hawaiian."

"Pizza and bed. Make that hot shower, pizza, and bed. Tonight's version of heaven," she smiled. "It's the little pleasures you treasure."

She headed for the kitchen. Petty officer Pritchett approached. "Hey Swanson, you must be living right. According to the pump, I put a half-gallon more in the tank than it should hold. You're lucky you aren't sitting a few miles offshore bobbing around like a cork."

Kristi smiled. *Thank you, my friend, for bringing me home safe. Now, where's the pizza?*

Two

Kristi lay in bed, not wanting to acknowledge the morning. It was Saturday, and she would be relieved by the weekend duty section. She rolled her head from side to side, then stretched her arms and legs like a kitten. She pulled herself into a sitting position and put her feet on the floor. She stretched again, padded to the toilet, removed her pajamas, and threw them on the bed. She didn't usually wear pajamas at home but wore them when she slept over on duty nights. The duty rooms were private and had locked doors, but she felt safer when completely covered here. Besides, you never knew when someone would get you out of bed in the middle of the night.

It was early, and she took her time going through her morning routine. She left the duty room by 6:35. The relief would be here by 7. Then, she'd be able to leave and enjoy her weekend. But she planned to stay around, at least for a few hours, to write her report and make sure everything was going smoothly for the Saturday crew. When Vince Ayala, the previous senior non-commissioned officer, left, she became the acting senior NCO. It had been a lot of responsibility. After a year away, Vince was back. That was nice, but she still felt responsible for the station.

She entered the small kitchen adjacent to the duty rooms, grabbed a cup from the shelf, and dropped a k-cup into the single-cup coffee maker. She smiled. Gone were the days of coming into the kitchen to a pot of coffee that had been cooking all night. She hated drinking sludge. She checked the refrigerator and pulled out a dozen eggs. She grabbed a skillet, sprayed it, put it on the induction cooktop, and broke an egg into it.

She was putting two slices of bread into the toaster when she heard a voice behind her.

"Hey. Mind throwing another egg in there? I'll do the pan." It was McPherson, his red hair going in all directions. He slumped into a seat at a small table.

"Uh, yeah. Sure," she said and broke another egg into the pan. "You know, your timing is always perfect. You appear just after I've started. Every time." She put two more pieces of bread into the toaster.

"A gift. It's the thing I do best in life."

"I'm sure that's not true. But – you're going to have to learn to cook one of these days."

"I can cook," he said.

"Milk and cereal isn't cooking. By the way, have you seen Pritchett this morning?"

"Yeah. He took off about 6:30. Said he had an appointment. Figured nothing would happen before we turned over the watch."

"He's technically, no, not technically, actually UA. He could be written up. That guy is almost less than worthless sometimes."

"Yeah, well, from what I understand, he's out at the end of this enlistment. He's failed to be promoted, and his evals don't look good. Only a miracle could keep him in," he said.

"ROAD program," she said, "retired on active duty." The toaster popped, and she grabbed the toast, slathered the slices with butter, then slid the fried eggs onto them. She plopped the sandwiches on paper plates and handed one to McPherson. Before covering her egg with the second piece of toast, she salted and peppered it, then offered the seasonings to him. He refused with a shake of his head as he took a quarter of the sandwich with one bite.

"Morning folks," came a voice from the door. They turned to see Vince Ayala, the senior non-commissioned officer.

"Morning," said Kristi, smiling.

McPherson mumbled something that could have been 'Good morning' if his mouth hadn't been full of egg sandwich.

"How was your night?"

McPherson finally swallowed. "Kristi had quite an evening."

"Oh? How so?"

"Some moron took his family out in that storm last night," he said. "Apparently hit some flotsam and started to sink. Kristi took a boat out and managed to find them just before all three went down with the ship."

"Congratulations," he said. "Tell me more." He pulled the used k-cup from the coffee maker, inserted another, and placed a cup under the spigot before starting the brew.

"Not much to tell," she said. "I went out, looked around, and finally found them."

"Alone?"

"Uh, yeah," she said, sipping her coffee. She turned and set her plate on the table and started to clean the skillet.

"Don't clean it. I'll make one for myself," Vince said.

"I can do it. No trouble," she said, looking away. "Besides, when I'm done with this one, McPherson is going to do the dishes."

Vince looked at McPherson, who only shrugged.

She broke an egg into the pan and placed two pieces of bread into the toaster.

"So, alone?" he asked again.

"Uh, yeah," she said, concentrating more than she needed to on the frying egg.

"Why alone?"

"McPherson was on a hospital run. Supplies. He thought it would be a good time. You know, no idiot would go out in a storm like this. Go figure. Pritchett had to stay and crew the station. That left me."

"And I got called out for a special assignment," he said as his coffee finished brewing. He took a sip. "You couldn't wait until McPherson got back?" It was a question, not a criticism.

"The mayday was pretty desperate. I was afraid that if I didn't go immediately," she let the rest die out. "McPherson wouldn't have been back for more than a half an hour. I couldn't wait that long."

The toast and egg were both done. She buttered the toast and dropped it onto a paper plate, slid the egg onto it, and seasoned it lightly before handing it to Vince with a smile.

"Thank you," he said, then he took a bite. "Perfect," he added. He set the plate on the table. "So, how far out were they?" he asked, sipping his coffee.

"Uh, about ten miles," she said quietly.

"Ten miles? In that storm?"

"Pritchett said she was running on less than fumes when she got back," added McPherson.

Kristi shot him a dirty look.

"So, you almost ran out of fuel? In that storm?" Vince asked.

"I know I broke a few rules. I shouldn't have done that, but I couldn't let them go down on that boat." *I shouldn't tell him*

I was scared to death the whole time, she thought. "I think they had another ten minutes – tops – when I got there."

Vince sat and stared at her. "If you were a guy, I'd tell you that was an incredibly stupid thing to do. Incredibly brave but incredibly stupid. You're lucky to be alive. But you saved three lives. You can be proud of that."

"Since I'm not a guy?" she asked.

"Same damn thing. Good work. I'm glad it worked out, and you got back here safe." He sipped his coffee. "Also, glad I didn't know about it at the time. As I said, you can be proud of that."

Something warm pulsed inside her. She'd taken a chance, and it went well. And recognition by Vince.

He looked at the clock. "Time for the turnover. Where's Pritchett?"

"Uh, he said he had an appointment and had to leave about 6:30," said McPherson.

"Jesus! That guy is less than worthless."

"You took the words right out of Kristi's mouth," said McPherson.

"I'll have to chew his ass for this. Enter it in the log."

"Will do," said McPherson.

"You guys headed out?" asked Vince.

"Yeah," said McPherson. "I've got a date with a long nap and a couple of cold ones."

"I'm going to stay here for a bit," said Kristi, "and finish my report. It was late, and I was tired. I only made some notes."

"You could use some rest, too," said Vince. "Oh, don't forget we've got the PFT on Tuesday. The OIC won't be here, and I'll need you two to help me administer it."

McPherson was walking away, mumbling something and waving his right hand in the air above his head as he walked.

"Gonna do it as before?" she asked. "Swim off to see who pays?"

"No. I'll pay. You and I will have a swim-off to see who cleans up after," he said, smiling.

Oh, great, she thought. *I guess the women will clean. No way I can beat him.* "Damn!" she said.

"What?" he asked.

"McPherson left without doing the skillet. Again."

Vince laughed. "I'll do it. You fixed breakfast. It's the least I can do."

He took the pan from her, and their hands touched. Her face warmed as old emotions smoldered. "Thank you," she said, not allowing herself to look at him.

Three

Kristi hit the 'print' box on the computer screen, yawned, and stretched. The three-page report on the rescue last night printed out. She picked it up and started reading through it, checking for typographical errors and places where her description of the event could be clearer. She wanted it to be perfect. It was her third try. *Thank God for computers*, she thought. She couldn't imagine having to type all the copies, then type them again when she found errors. After reviewing, she decided this copy should be good enough to file electronically. She'd still send a hard copy up the local chain of command. Maybe she'd have Vince take a look before she sent something she couldn't recover.

She picked up the report and headed to his office. Vince was sitting at his desk, looking at some paperwork. She knocked on the doorframe.

"Oh, hi," he said. "I thought you'd be gone by now."

"I just finished the report and wanted you to look at it before I send it up the chain. I'm having a little trouble getting my thoughts together this morning. Let me know if anything is unclear." She handed him the report and turned to leave.

"Have a seat," he said, motioning to the empty armchair angled toward his desk.

She took a seat, and he started to review the report. "Coffee?" he asked.

"Uh, yeah, sure. I could go and make it," she said.

"I'll make it," he said, turning to the one-cupper on the counter behind him.

"Coming up in the world," she said with a smile. "Now you've got your own coffee mess."

"Had to buy it myself, but it saves the walk to the kitchen." He dropped a k-cup into the machine, grabbed a clean cup from a cupboard, slid it into place, and pushed the start button. He began to review the report as the coffee brewed. When the coffee was done, he added a bit of Splenda and creamer. He handed her the cup, saying, "Bon appetite." Then, he returned to the report. After a few minutes, he looked up.

"Nice report. Good rescue. I'd feel better if two of you had gone out, but I understand your reasoning. Sorry I wasn't here to back you up."

"Not your fault. It worked out."

"Yeah," he said, "three people are alive because it worked out. Go ahead and submit it. It looks good."

"Thank you," she said and left to submit the electronic version. Twenty minutes later, Kristi was ready to leave but felt like staying a little longer. She changed into civilian clothes and stopped at Vince's office.

"I'm going to head out," she said, "unless you need me for something else."

"Uh, no. But I'd like to chat if you've got a few minutes."

"Sure," she said, entering and dropping into an overstuffed chair. "What's on your mind?"

He handed her a sheet of paper. "That's my plan for the PFT," he said. Take a look and let me know what you think."

She studied the page. "Looks good to me. Anything else?"

"I was just wondering about your plans for the future. Have you thought about what you want that to look like?"

"I don't know. I guess I'd like to make chief. Get my retirement." She paused and looked at the floor. "I joined because things were tough at home. My mom was a teacher. Dad drove a truck. They made ends meet, but there wasn't a lot left over. One day, my dad drove off and didn't come back. He didn't die or anything. I guess he just wanted to be somewhere else."

Vince sat quietly.

"The Coast Guard gave me a way to relieve Mom of some of the money strain. That way, I wasn't a liability, and I was able to send some money home to help out. And, it got me started on a career."

"Sounds like a lot of responsibility," he said.

"Well, it wasn't heroic. It was a practical solution." She paused and sipped her coffee. "I don't want to have to depend on someone else. Someone else can always leave, and then," she looked at him, "you're screwed."

"Someone else doesn't always leave."

"But you don't know, do you? Besides, I'll be able to retire before I'm forty. Then, I can find something else. I'll have my safety net. Maybe I'll even be important."

"Have you given any thought to going after a commission?" he asked.

"Me?"

"Yes, you. You've done very well here. Senior NCO while I was away. You're dedicated to the mission and station. The decision to go out last night wasn't an easy one. You could have sent someone else, but you didn't."

"What does that have to do," she started.

"You handle responsibility very well. You take on challenges. My opinion is that you'd make an outstanding officer."

"I – I don't even know how. I mean, what would I do?"

"All I'm asking is that you give it some thought. There are programs where you could continue to do your current work and work toward a commission. Or, they might pay you to go to school full time. You'd do well. The money is better, and so is the retirement."

It was Kristi's turn to sit quietly.

"Think about it. We can talk later about the steps to get there. Now, why don't you go enjoy what's left of your weekend?"

Kristi left the office and headed to the parking lot. She looked out at the ocean. *An officer? Me? Lieutenant Swanson. Commander Swanson? How about Captain Swanson?* She smiled, and an electric tingle ran through her. *It wouldn't hurt to check, would it?*

Four

On Monday morning, Kristi stood at attention in front of the OIC's desk. Lieutenant Commander Kaye Christianson had been the officer in charge of Sandy Bay for six months. She had not endeared herself to the rank-and-file enlisted personnel at the Coast Guard Station during that time. One reason was her demand that any enlisted personnel reporting to her had to stand at attention in front of her desk for the entire meeting. She'd even taped a box on the floor where she wanted them to stand while she held court.

Kristi was doing a slow burn. She had been summoned, and the OIC was questioning her actions of Friday night. Another officer, a lieutenant commander, who wasn't stationed at Sandy Bay, was sitting in the office. His headquarters nametag read, "Bond."

"So, Petty Officer Swanson," Christianson started, "run me through what happened Friday night."

"It's all in my report, ma'am."

"Yes. I see the report. I want your version in your own words."

"It was about 8:30."

"8:37 according to this report."

Kristi paused to get control of herself. She didn't want to get on the wrong side of her senior, but clearly, the officer was out to bully her. "That's the time in the log, yes, ma'am."

"Continue."

"The weather was pretty bad. Heavy rain and winds. We received a distress call. We couldn't determine the position accurately."

"Why?"

"They didn't know exactly where they were. They didn't have GPS, and radar wasn't particularly useful because of the high seas. Small boat and all. They weren't on long enough to triangulate their exact position, but they said they had hit something and were taking on water."

"Go on."

"I took one of the response boats and headed out to look for them. An air search was not possible because of the weather. I believe there were a couple of other craft in the area looking for them too."

Christianson closed the report and placed it on the desk. "You took the boat out alone." It was an accusation. "Against instructions and general orders."

"Yes, ma'am. Pritchett had to stay at the station and monitor the radio. McPherson was on his way back from the hospital, and I didn't know how long he would be. I didn't want to take a chance on people drowning. The man radioing stated his wife and daughter were aboard."

"Still. Another thing. Instructions state you are to return to the base when you hit your reserve. According to others, your tanks were bone dry when you returned."

Pritchett. "Yes, I was running low, as you say, ma'am, but I reached the sinking vessel just about the time I started into the reserve fuel. And, a boat that normally has two feet of freeboard was down to six inches, or so, with water washing over the transom. I don't think they would have stayed afloat much longer. I would hate to think of that little girl, especially, drowning. The station and Coast Guard will receive credit for the rescue."

"Yes, it was a commendable rescue, but such grandstanding could have had you stranded in the middle of the Pacific. We might have lost you and the boat. That wouldn't play well for the station or the Coast Guard. You would do well to remember that. General orders and instructions exist for a reason. Next time, obey them. By the way, where was Chief Ayala during all this?"

"Yes, ma'am. The chief got a call from headquarters Thursday. He was told to report up there. He was still gone at the time of the call."

"And you or he didn't think that was important for me to know?"

"I would have thought that they would have informed you if headquarters wanted him for something. Or he would have done so – Ma'am."

The delay in Kristi's use of 'ma'am' now had Christianson's face tinged with red. "Very well. I may want to talk with you later." She picked put the report and tossed it on the front of the desk. "Take that to Miss Duncan for filing. Dismissed."

Kristi picked up the folder, did an about-face, and left the office, closing the door more firmly than necessary.

Christianson sat back in her chair and turned to the other officer in the room. "So. What do you think?"

"What she did was actually pretty brave," said Bond. He was watching Kristi's body as she walked out of view. He hid the lust he was feeling. *Too bad she's off-limits*, he thought. *That might be fun.* Then, he turned to her. "She could have been killed. It could have been setup, you know, drug runners. Something like that. You might go easy on her. Even praise her, although you don't seem like you want to do that."

"Little perky blond. I want her to know who is in charge. The only good thing about being here is that nobody questions my authority. It's nice to have that power. But being here doesn't do me any good. I'm stuck out in this Podunk rescue station when I'd rather be up at headquarters. That's where I'm going to get in front of people who can get me promoted. Advance my career."

"Yes, that's true, but having this operational tour will give you a leg up." He paused. "You know, I think we can work this to your advantage. Write something for Swanson. Nothing big. Maybe a letter of appreciation. We'll get a photo op. Show you giving it to her. Feature you more than her. I can even slip it into conversations with the higher-ups that though it may have been a risky mission, your leadership has inspired your team to go above and beyond."

"Thank you," said Christianson.

"Who is this Chief Ayala?" asked Bond.

"Senior NCO," said Christianson. "He was here before I got here. They pulled him for some special assignment. Hush-hush. Now, he's back, but they keep pulling him. He gets a call from headquarters, and he goes. They don't tell me when or what for. That little comment from Swanson pissed me off, but it was on the mark. How dare they take one of mine and not tell me."

"Maybe I can find out something. I'll check around."

"You think so? Okay. Thank you. I appreciate it," she said.

"We can get ahead faster if we work as a team. Working our way up the ladder works better if two or three people work together. I'm sure that when you can help me out, you will. We'll both be successful together. Making each other look good doesn't seem self-serving if we do it for someone else. Don't worry. We'll get there."

"I want to get there as fast as possible," she said. "Then, I can live in civilization. Live in a place with real restaurants and real entertainment. And have a better chance of a real job with real potential and real money after I retire. My philosophy is to get one retirement and start working on the second. And make the most of each."

"For me," he said, "the retirement is enough. It's a safety net that allows me to do whatever I want. But I'm not worried about money, and you don't have to wait, at least not for the money."

"How so?"

"I've got a couple of friends. They're fans of the service. He couldn't serve himself. Medical issue, I think. Filthy rich. They've got connections. They've let me put money into an investment business they have. The returns are incredible."

"What's the deal?" she asked.

"They use clients' money to leverage their investments. Venture capital, I think. They want to keep it quiet, but I could probably talk them into letting you in. My returns have been 25 percent or greater. It's incredible. And, I'm sure they could help you after you leave the service. They've got a lot of influential friends. Many as investors. They could help with your career goals. Doesn't hurt to have friends. They're having a dinner next Friday. I get a plus one. Why don't you come along?"

"Sure. Why not? I can always use a free dinner."

Five

Kristi walked to the office in the back corner of the old hangar. Annie, the station's civilian administrative assistant, sat behind her desk, concentrating on stacks of paperwork. File cabinets covered the right side of the small office. A single cup coffee maker on a cabinet and a small refrigerator were on the left side.

The door was open, but Kristi knocked on the side panel anyway.

"Oh, hi," said Annie, looking up. "Come on in."

"The commander wanted me to drop this off," said Kristi, handing her the report.

"Nice bit of work," said Annie.

"Not according to her. She thinks it could put the station and Coast Guard in a bad light."

"You're kidding."

"Nope. Had me at attention and essentially dressed me down."

"Probably because her name isn't all over it as the heroine of the day. And not that she'd ever do anything heroic."

"The thing that made me mad was that she did it in front of another officer. One assigned to headquarters. I mean, I know maybe I should have waited for McPherson to return, but,"

"Oh, yeah. Bond. They're chummy. He's in admin up at HQ. I've dealt with him a couple of times. Kind of a cold prickly. Pretty much interested in himself and his career. Hey! You saved three lives."

"Why's he here, then?" asked Kristi.

Annie motioned to the chair next to her desk. "Have a seat. I think they've decided to team up. Help each other with their careers. Climbers. They brainstorm about strategies for dinner parties. Who they can butter up and how they can do it best. All that stuff. They plan to make captain as soon as possible."

"Probably sleeping together."

Annie cocked her head and thought a few seconds. "No. If they are, it's just sleeping, and what's the fun in that?"

"How do you know?" asked Kristi.

"Uh, just a feeling. I'm usually right."

"She got all upset when I told her Ayala had been pulled. Wanted to know why HQ hadn't told her. If they didn't tell her, they wouldn't tell me. I don't know why they wouldn't tell her, though."

"I don't know, either," said Annie, "and I've got a pretty good network. All I know is that he gets a call – mid-afternoon usually, during the week – from a Petty Officer Amy Way. Like this last time. The conversation lasts about ten seconds, and he disappears."

"Petty Officer Way? Do you know where she works?"

"No. The call came in here once," she said, nodding to her phone. "She identified herself and asked for the chief. I told her he was out on the water and asked if I could take a message. She said "No," and hung up. I waited a few minutes and hit the call back on the phone. A guy answered, and all he said was the phone number. No hello. No "this is." Nothing. I kinda went, "Uh," and he asked what extension number I wanted. I mumbled that I must have dialed wrong, and he just hung up. No 'Bye, have a nice day,' nothing. It was weird, but I haven't tried calling back. I get the feeling they don't want any calls."

"That is weird. I'd like to know what it's about. It's a cinch they aren't telling Christianson, either."

"Sometimes, it's best not to know," said Annie.

Kristi shook her head as if trying to shake the last conversation free. "Vince came in Saturday morning. We spent some time talking about where I am in my career. My plans. He asked me where I see myself in a few years—that game. I said I wasn't sure. I was just throwing out ideas. He encouraged me to look into applying for a commission. I might. Look into it, that is. Find out what I'd need. I don't know."

"So, how are you two doing?" asked Annie.

"What do you mean?"

"Before he left, you two were dating."

27

"Yeah, well, that was before. Now he's my boss, and the Coast Guard doesn't like seniors and juniors in the same chain of command dating. Besides, I'm not sure where we are, with or without the prohibition. I mean, if we were at different commands, would he be interested?"

"Are you?" Annie asked.

"I just don't want to put my heart on the line just to have it broken."

"Well, unfortunately, there's only one way to really find out."

"Besides, I can't afford to destroy my career."

"Back to this commission thing," said Annie.

"It would be a good career path. Success and respect. A little more money, too. But I'm not sure I have what it takes," said Kristi.

"I think you have what it takes. I've seen a lot of officers. You're as competent as they are. Better than a lot of them on other scales. But success and respect? You've got that."

"Yeah, well, last time I was back home, family and friends didn't exactly swoon when I said I was a first class petty officer in the Coast Guard. It would be nice to make them "wow" a little. Besides, I hate standing in that little box in front of Christianson's desk. I'd like to be in a position to rip that thing off. But I wanted to talk to you about it. You've been around here for a while."

"Thanks. You make me sound old. I'm not much older than you are," said Annie.

"Sorry. I didn't mean it that way. It's just – you have connections and know what's going on."

"That's better."

"No. I mean, you kind of know the ins and outs of things. You're always on top of stuff."

"Obviously," said Annie, gesturing to the piles of paper on her desk.

"Well, they couldn't run this place without you. I think you-know-who offloads her administrative work onto you," said Kristi.

"I know she does. So, what do you want to know?"

"If I apply, I want to know how to put my application in the best light. To give me the best shot. Not that I've decided. I'm just wondering."

"I'm not sure I know how to do that. Have you talked to the career counselors up at headquarters?"

"They give out the standard spiel. Usually give you a URL to get information online. Maybe they're afraid of being called on favoritism if they give one person extra information. I want more than the usual. Improve my chances if I decide. You know."

"Well, you might try Commander Cruise. I think the San Lorenzo is in port this week. Give her a call, or send an e-mail.

29

I'm sure she'd see you, and she's always happy to help people – good people – people she knows – progress in their careers."

"I don't know. She's the captain of a cutter. An officer. She's got her own," started Kristi.

"God! You'll have to learn to push if you plan on going for a commission." Annie picked up the phone and consulted her mobile.

"I don't know," said Kristi. "I mean, is this considered going outside my chain of command?"

Annie punched a few numbers and waited. "Hi! Is the captain available? This is Annie Duncan from Sandy Bay calling. Thanks." She covered the phone and turned to Kristi, "They're checking. Should only be – Hi! Dee. How's it going? Uh-huh. Uh-huh. Sounds fun. Listen, Dee, I have Kristi Swanson in my office." Pause. "It's first class now." Annie covered the phone and turned to Kristi, "Congratulations." She uncovered the phone, "So, Kristi is thinking about applying for a commission. Yup. But she'd like to talk to someone unofficially about what she can do to increase her chances of acceptance. I suggested you. Well, I think so. Friday? About noon. Perfect. I'll let her know. By the way, how's Scott?" Annie laughed. "Well, it takes two to tango. It isn't just his fault if you're getting worn out when you're in port. Good to talk. Let's get together. Okay. Bye." Annie hung up. "So, next Friday at noon. Long Beach Harbor. You're welcome."

"Thank you. Now all I have to do is figure out what I want to ask her," said Kristi.

"I can only do so much for you. I'm sure you'll be fine. Remember, she's a great person and ready to help someone she knows."

Six

Vince Ayala pulled his red 1957 Ford Thunderbird into the "Senior NCO" spot and turned off the engine. Early morning and the day was warming already. He rolled his head and tried to shake the fatigue from his body. He opened the door and pulled himself out. Before closing the door, he retrieved a leather bag from the passenger's seat. He rotated his left arm, checking it after his recent injury.

He walked around to the large opening in the former seaplane hangar. Along the right wall were the OIC's office, his small office, records storage, the civilian assistant's office, and sickbay in the rear. The back of the hangar held tools and parts storage, equipment, and a workout room. The left side contained an operations center, the male locker room, a lounge and kitchenette, three small duty rooms, and the female locker room. Cool, almost cold, fresh air greeted him as he entered. Two watercraft, partially disassembled, were in the large hangar bay.

His heels clicked on the concrete floor as he started toward his office. He saw Kristi Swanson leaving the admin office. Kristi Swanson. Blond. Beautiful. Intelligent and professional. They'd dated when his good friend Scott Jackson had been the senior NCO. He remembered how it felt to hold her. He missed that and the warm feeling that came with it. Scott retired – quickly – and married the former OIC, Dee Cruise. Dee was promoted rapidly, held the rank of commander, and was now captain of a Coast Guard cutter, the San Lorenzo.

Ayala made chief during a year hiatus and was given his choice of orders when that tour ended. He chose to return to Sandy Bay. Now he was Kristi's supervisor, and they couldn't keep dating. It wasn't the officer–enlisted prohibition that Scott and Dee had violated, but it was still a superior-subordinate relationship frowned upon by the service. He didn't think either of them was happy about it. He wasn't, that was for sure. But neither of them wanted to run afoul of the service, and neither was at a point where they could retire. There was no Scott Jackson solution for them. Since then, he'd tried to ignore his feelings and kept to himself.

"Hey, chief!"

Ayala turned to see Scott McPherson striding up.

"Decided to see if the place is still running?" McPherson asked.

"You have the OIC to make sure things go as planned."

"Yeah. You know as well as I do, she's just here for a ticket punch. She's admin all the way. Couldn't run an op if she had to."

"That's no way to talk about the OIC," Ayala said without conviction. "So, who's been holding the place together?"

"Like you don't know. Swanson. Been doing it since you left. Made that incredible rescue Friday night. I don't think the OIC was happy about it, though. Swanson came out of the OIC's office and headed for Annie's. It looked like she was pissed. The commander must have given her a ration about something."

"I'm surprised you don't have the whole story. Not much escapes you. I'm not sure how you do it, though."

"My little secret. Some people, including you, can get the what. I never reveal who tells me."

Ayala turned his attention to the blond heading for the operations center. "Petty Officer Swanson!"

Kristi stopped and turned. When she saw him, she said, "Yes, chief?"

"See you a minute?"

McPherson sauntered off. Vince walked into his office and stood waiting for her. Inside was a desk, two chairs, and an aged leather couch. They entered, and Ayala opened the top of a single cup coffee maker.

"What do you like?" he asked, opening a cabinet stocked with k-cups.

"French roast."

He dropped the k-cup into the machine and started it.

"You okay?" he asked.

"Yeah. OIC chewed my ass this morning for that rescue."

34

"Chewed your ass? For saving three people?"

Her coffee finished brewing. He added a bit of cream and half a Splenda, then handed her the cup.

She took the coffee and shrugged her shoulders. "Well, we were shorthanded."

"You should get a commendation."

"Not to hear Christianson tell it. According to her, I violated enough regulations and instructions to get a reprimand. And, I did break some rules."

"I'll have a word with her. I've got an idea she just wants to play everything safe until she can get out of here and back to a safe, warm administrative position where she can push papers around all day and have weekends off. In her book, it's better to play safe and lose lives – not hers, of course – so her record is clean. You did a great job. You might have bent a couple of regs, but three people are alive because of it. No matter what else, you should be proud of that."

"Thank you. I was beginning to wonder," she said.

"But I was thinking," he said, "that boat, the Francine, should never have been out under those conditions. It makes no sense. Day sailor going ten miles out at night in a storm. I'd like to talk to the guy who thought it would be a good idea. You up for a little trip?"

"Robert Johnson? Sure. Why not?" she answered.

"Why don't we start with his wife?" Vince paused. "Another thing. They're pulling me away a couple of times

35

every week, and I know you're the one keeping this place together while I'm gone. I appreciate that. Your next eval will be a water walker."

"Until she gets it, that is," said Kristi. "I don't suppose you can tell me what big hush-hush thing is they have you doing."

"No. It's no big deal, really, but for some reason, they want to keep it on the QT. I wish I could. You understand," he said. "I know it's hurting operations. I'm sorry."

"If they pull you, it isn't your fault."

"I'm supposed to be the one in charge," he said.

"Actually, she's in charge. She's the one responsible. She's the one who should be raising morale."

"Well, I think we both know that isn't going to happen." He paused and looked at her.

"Understood. Never said. Never heard."

Seven

Vince verified the address, left the car, walked around to the passenger side, and opened the door for Kristi. They checked their uniforms, walked to the front door of the large French country home, and knocked.

A petite brown-haired woman wearing a pale blue shirtwaist dress opened the door. Kristi recognized her as Margaret Johnson, the woman she'd rescued from the sinking pleasure craft during the storm at the end of April. Margaret was wiping her hands on a towel. When she saw Kristi, she smiled.

"Hello. Please come in," she said. She opened the door wide and led them to the living room. "Please sit. Would you like something to drink? I've just made some cookies."

"Uh, sure," said Kristi, "anything is fine."

A few minutes later, she brought a plate full of cookies and a pot of coffee.

"Now," she said, "I'm sure this is more than a social call. How can I help you?"

"Well," started Vince, "we were trying to determine what happened the night during the storm. I need to put the finishing touches on the report. As you can probably guess, official reports have to be complete. As it is, there may be a question or two later. Can you tell us what you remember of that night?"

"I don't know how much I can tell you," she said.

"Just start at the beginning," said Kristi. "Tell us everything you remember."

"Well, I didn't think we were going out on the boat that night. I'd planned dinner, but when Bob came home, he said he wanted to take the boat up the coast. I thought it was strange. We didn't use the boat after sunset, but Bob was adamant when I voiced my reluctance. He seemed very nervous. He said it would be fun. When I finally agreed, he seemed to relax."

She took a sip of her coffee. "So, we got ready to go, but Bob kept checking his watch. He wasn't in a hurry, then he was. Like he had a schedule. So, we went off to the marina. Bob drove so fast. He even ran a couple of lights. I asked what the hurry was, and he said something about tides. I guess we had to go out when the tides were right. I don't know anything about boats or boating myself."

"What time was that, Mrs. Johnson?" asked Vince.

"I think we left about seven. Bob headed out using the compass. I asked him if it would be better to stay close to the shore so he could make sure we wouldn't get lost, but he said it wouldn't be a problem."

"Was there anything else?" asked Kristi.

"Yes. He made sure we had our life jackets on the entire time. He checked a couple of times. That was different. He's never done that before."

"And you headed out to sea?"

"Yes, away from shore. He kept checking his watch. I didn't understand. Amber and I were nervous and stayed huddled in the stern."

"So, did you feel whatever your husband hit?"

"No. He asked me to steer the boat and keep the compass needle pointed where it was. He pointed to where I was supposed to keep the needle pointing. He said it over and over to make sure I understood. It was heading two eight zero."

"Did he tell you the heading or just point to the compass?" asked Kristi.

"He just pointed. Then he went to the head. He came back a couple of minutes later. About five minutes later, he turned around with a worried look and said, 'Did you feel that?' I didn't feel anything."

"Did either you or your daughter use the marine toilet that night?" asked Vince.

"No. We went before we left the marina. Bob always wants us to do that. He was in a hurry that night and told us to use the public toilet but to make it quick. The one on the boat has all kinds of valves, and you have to pump it out. If we use it, Bob does whatever to fill it, and then we use it. He pumps it out. We're scared to use it by ourselves. Even if we try, he always checks to make sure everything is closed, the valves, I guess, after we've finished. No. Neither Amber nor I used the toilet."

"Okay. Can you tell us what happened after your husband thought he'd hit something?"

"Uh, Sure. We kind of sailed along for a bit. I thought if we'd hit something, maybe we should head for shore. At least get in sight of it. He said there shouldn't be a problem. But before very long, there was a problem. He said whatever we'd hit must have damaged the hull because we were beginning to take on water."

She sipped her coffee.

"By that time," she continued, "it was dark, and the storm had come up. Bob was starting to look worried, and he went down into the cabin to assess the damage. He was back in a minute. He said he couldn't stop it. That's when he made the first call on the radio – for help. I could tell he was worried then. I tried to be as brave as possible, but I was scared stiff. I couldn't understand what was so important about going out that night – I mean, we don't do boating at night. We barely do it during the day." She paused. "And so far from shore."

"Is there anything else you can tell us?" asked Vince.

"It wasn't long before the engine quit. And the auto bailers won't work unless you are moving. I guess the water did something. Then, Bob got really scared. He tried to hide it, but I could tell. He kept radioing for help, but when we finally got an answer, he didn't know where we were exactly. The boat kept sinking. I don't think we would have lasted much longer when," she looked at Kristi, "you arrived. Thank God! If you hadn't gotten there, I just don't know what we would have done." A tear was running down her cheek. After a minute, she composed herself. "I want to thank you again. We're probably alive because you saved us. It was stupid for us to be out there."

Vince drained his coffee and stood. "Thank you for your time and the information, Mrs. Johnson. If we need anything else, I hope we can see you again."

"Anything you folks need. Anything. I'll be more than happy."

Vince headed to the door. Mrs. Johnson hugged Kristi and began talking to her. Thinking it might be private, he headed to the car. Ten minutes later, Kristi joined him.

"Well, that was interesting," she said.

"How do you mean? More than an outpouring of gratitude?"

"Yes. More. It seems Mr. Johnson has a gambling problem. He was in over his head, but after that night, he said he'd learned what was important in life and swore off.

"Interesting," said Vince, "Still, I'd like to know why a casual day boater decided to go far out to sea at night and during that storm."

"And, I wonder if he's counting on insurance money to pay off his gambling debts," she said.

"Good thought. We should talk with Mr. Johnson."

He held the door for Kristi, then got into the driver's side, and they headed off.

Vince looked at Kristi, who looked lost in thought. "Problem?" he asked.

"I don't know. Just something nagging in the back of my mind. I can't quite put my finger on it."

Eight

That afternoon, they sat across the table from Bob Johnson in a small glass-enclosed meeting room in the bank where he worked as a manager.

"So, what can I do for the Coast Guard today?" he asked.

"We just need to go over a few things for our report," said Vince.

"I thought that was all taken care of," he said, shifting in his chair.

"Well, because you reported this as an accident, the insurance company wants us to file a detailed report." He paused. "Nothing worse than the government and the insurance industry in a combined effort," he said.

"Oh, right."

"So, can we start with why you decided to go out that night? From all indications, you're pretty much a day sailor. Night is different."

"I had a client up the coast. He wanted to meet and invited me up. I'd told him about my boat, and he said I should bring it up. He was staying at a resort. Said he'd had an extra room comped and I should bring my wife and daughter. He said it would be a great weekend. I thought it would be, too. So, I agreed." Johnson was sweating slightly.

"Okay. Good. Now, your wife said," started Vince.

"You talked to my wife?" Johnson asked defensively.

"Um, yeah. It's routine in accidents to talk to everyone. Sometimes one person will remember something the other doesn't," said Vince.

"Oh, yeah, I guess so. Just surprised me, is all."

"You okay?" asked Vince. When Johnson nodded, he continued. "Your wife said you seemed to be in a great hurry. Kept checking your watch."

"Yeah. The appointment was for nine. I didn't want to be late."

"Sure. That makes sense. So, you got underway about seven. Instead of hugging the coast, you decided to head out farther to sea. I mean, Petty Officer Swanson found you about," he shuffled through some papers, "just over ten miles out. That's a long way, especially if you're not used to boating at night."

"And with the storm coming up," added Kristi.

"So, I mean, what? This is beginning to sound like an interrogation."

"I'm sorry if we sound like we're accusing, but our superiors want information. You have to admit, the trip was ill-considered. We just want to hear your side of the story," said Vince.

"Okay," he said, rubbing the back of his neck with his hand, "yes, we were farther out than I thought. I thought going out a little farther and swinging north would be quicker. I had to go to the head, and I had my wife steer for a bit. I didn't check the compass when I got back – that was my mistake, I can see that now – and I think she put us off course. She knows nothing about boats."

"And, then, you hit something in the water. Or, it hit you," offered Vince.

"Yeah. Maybe it did hit me. I never thought of that."

"When you noticed you were taking on water," said Kristi, "was there a reason you didn't turn toward shore?"

"I didn't think we were that far out, but you're right. I should have turned toward shore as soon as I noticed the water. I guess I was still hoping to make the resort. I knew heading for shore would mean we'd miss the weekend. But the flooding was worse than I thought."

"And then?" asked Vince.

"The engine died, and I realized we were in real trouble. I radioed for help. It seems like it took forever."

"You couldn't give a position?" asked Vince.

"I'm not as good a navigator as I thought," he said, looking at the table.

"And you're sure you hit something in the water."

"Yes. I felt it. I'm sure it cracked the hull. I only wish we could prove that. But the boat is probably sitting in a thousand feet of water. No way to," he stopped. Then, "And if this brave young lady hadn't arrived, I don't know," he let the sentence die.

Nine

It was Tuesday morning, and Kristi stood inside the hangar, shivering in her dark blue sweatsuit. The sun had been up for an hour, but it still seemed cold. She was trying to warm herself before the fitness test.

"Good morning," she heard and turned to see Annie Duncan walking to her.

"Oh, hi, Annie," she responded.

"Cold?"

"Uh, yeah. Some. Once the sun heats the place, it will be better." Kristi looked at Annie. She was competent and professional but also known to have a playful side. Sometimes Annie liked to do odd things just to see what would happen. Today, it was typical Annie, wearing a classic French sailor Breton top cut short above the waist, dark blue high-waisted palazzo pants, and a white French navy hat with a red pom-pom on top. Pulling it off perfectly. The picture of a petite French sailor – with curves.

Annie described herself in fours – size 4, five foot four, and 114 pounds. She would be easy to hate if she wasn't one of the sweetest people Kristi had ever met. They could have been sisters and had been mistaken for sisters. Both were blond, and both had attractive figures. Kristi was a bit taller at 5' 6," and her curves were slightly curvier. They'd each seen men walk into posts or walls while ogling them.

"If you want, we could get some hot tea in my office," said Annie.

"Thanks. That would be nice."

They walked to her office in silence. Kristi might have asked about Annie's outfit, but she wasn't sure how.

"So," started Kristi, "I wonder why work weeks seem to go so slowly, and then the weekend flies by."

"Just the way it works, I guess. What did you do Friday night?" asked Annie.

"I had the duty and had to go out on that rescue."

"Oh, yeah. Well, that explains Friday night. It was stormy."

"Yeah. I was happy to get back here safely."

"But, Saturday. Well, you would have slept over. I know you stayed for a while. What time did you get out of here Saturday?"

"After our watch was over, I stayed to finish my report on the rescue. Vince came in, so we talked. I guess I left about one," said Kristi.

"And you're asking why the weekend went so fast? You only had one day. Basically."

Annie put a tea module in the single-cup maker and asked, "What did you two talk about that kept you here until one on a Saturday? Other than your career. Or was it just a reason to spend time together? Have you given any more thought to how you feel?"

"I'm happy he came back here. I'm still sorting it all out. I think things could have gotten serious. Now, I don't know. Maybe we missed our chance." Kristi sipped her tea. "Mostly, we talked about my career. And, we talked about the PT test and how we'd handle the swim."

So, is there going to be a race to see who pays?"

"Uh, no. Vince, I mean Chief Ayala said he was going to buy," said Kristi.

"Oh, pooh!" said Annie.

"What?"

"I just like to watch the race. It was fun to see Scott Jackson come from behind then lose on purpose, so he would have to pay. He planned it that way every time. It was close a couple of times, but the race was fun. Beat Ayala the last year he was here."

"Yeah, well, there'll still be a race to see who cleans."

"Any idea who?" asked Annie.

"Yeah. I get to race Ayala. It looks like the ladies are going to be doing the cleaning."

"You're a good swimmer. You beat Pritchett."

"Yeah, well, Ayala is a much better swimmer than Pritchett," said Kristi.

"And," said Annie with a nod to Kristi's chest, "you've got a handicap. Olympic swimmers don't have boobs. The girls are going to slow you down."

"I don't think that will matter that much."

Annie had one eye closed and was looking heavenward with the other. "We could say it is an unfair match. Get him to wear a two-piece top filled with rocks."

Kristi just stared.

"Just a thought," said Annie, with a shrug.

"He might throw the race, give the ladies a break, but that wouldn't be fair," said Kristi.

"Screw fair," said Annie, just as a whistle blew, calling everyone to assemble.

They walked out of her office and to the growing assembly of Coast Guard personnel near the mouth of the hangar. Vince had a clipboard in his hands and was checking off names.

Ten

The test consisted of six parts. All had gone smoothly, and only the final test, a hundred-yard open water swim, was left. The swim wasn't timed, just out to a buoy in the bay and back. Completing the swim earned a passing mark. Vince and Kristi rode a jet ski pulling a sled. Kristi drove the ski, and Vince was behind her, ready to pull any swimmer who got into trouble out of the water. The staff were split up into groups of four.

The first group went in. A few sputtered, but no one was in real trouble. Kristi followed them out and back while Vince watched for any signs of distress. There were seven groups, and all completed the swim without incident. She pulled the jet ski to the dock and tied it up. Vince got off the sled and climbed onto the dock.

"Okay. Everyone did great. Congratulations. We've got a party scheduled for the rest of the day, and other stations in the area will take any calls, so you're free to have fun. Remember you still have to get home tonight and work tomorrow, so please temper any celebration with those things in mind."

A cheer went up.

"Petty officer Swanson and I will have the traditional swim competition to see whether the boys or the girls will do the party clean up."

Some of the men were smiling and congratulating themselves, figuring the chief would have an easy victory. Some of the women, likewise, were looking dejected.

Vince smiled at Kristi and said, "Shall we?"

She gave a weak smile and then pulled off her running shorts. Most of the men watched but tried not to show they were watching. Vince also watched Kristi closely while trying to look like he wasn't.

Vince left his t-shirt on and stepped out of his shoes. He grabbed two pairs of swim goggles and handed one to her. Then, they were off to the edge of the pier.

"Ready?" he asked.

"Sure," she replied and jumped into the water. Vince followed.

Kristi started at a decent pace, but he knew it wasn't her fastest. He was behind her a body length, matching her strokes.

She's saving her energy. Wondering when I'll make my move. She'll try to time it so I can't catch her. This should be fun. He watched the curve of her body and how she seemed to move effortlessly through the water. He felt a little guilty for what he was thinking. It wasn't all about her swimming prowess.

He stayed behind her until they reached the buoy. Kristi touched and turned, then splashed water at Vince with her hand. He laughed. She passed him and headed back as he neared the buoy.

He touched the buoy and started to turn. Something at the mouth of the bay caught his eye. It was just a quick change in the color of the water, from the blue-gray in the distance to a light gray. He paused and waited. In a few seconds, the color changed again. This time he saw movement. He started to swim slowly backward while keeping his eyes on the mouth of the bay. It happened a third time, only this time longer. A distinct gray body slid into his vision. Good sized. Ten, maybe twelve feet long. Aquadynamic. Dorsal fin. Vertical stripes along its side. A tiger shark. Edging closer.

He did a complete three-sixty without making a splash. He saw Kristi about a third of the way to the pier, swimming quickly. *I guess the guys will clean*, he thought, but that wasn't his main concern right now. He turned back to face the shark and paddled slowly backward toward the pier, keeping his eyes on the fish. It swam lazily, but it was slowly closing the distance between them.

Something touched his shoulder, and he jumped. He turned to see Kristi behind him.

"What are you doing here?" he said. "You should be back on shore."

"The people on the pier were pointing. I saw you weren't in the race and came to see what was so interesting," she said with a smile.

"Yeah, well, take a good look toward the mouth of the bay, and you'll see."

She dipped her head for a few seconds, then came back up. "That's a shark! A big shark!"

"Yeah. Which makes me want you on the pier. Come on."

She didn't move.

"Go!" he said.

She looked at him quickly, then started to swim rapidly.

He grabbed her ankle. She yelped.

"Slowly. Slowly. No splashing."

They began to stroke backward. The animal followed them, circling closer, turning away, then repeating the process. Each pass came a little closer. Vince kept himself between Kristi and the shark. He looked at her. Her eyes were huge.

It seemed like forever, but they were finally at the pier. He told her to leave the water first. She didn't argue. He waited until she was out. The shark made a pass, then turned away. As it did, he was up and out of the water. Somebody threw him a towel.

"So, who cleans after the party?" asked someone behind the group.

Before he could answer, Kristi spoke up. "Everybody. The race wasn't fair, and I know I don't want to do it over." She was wrapped in a towel.

Vince smiled and tilted his head in agreement. Then, "Okay, everyone, let's get this party underway!" A cheer went up.

"Buy you a drink?" he asked.

"Why thank you, but I should buy you one for getting me back safely," she answered, and they headed toward the hangar.

"You shouldn't have come back out," he said.

"I thought you might be in trouble. Are you saying that because I'm a girl?" she asked quietly and stared at him.

"No. I didn't want two people at risk," he lied. The truth was he didn't want *her* at risk.

Annie approached. "There was a call for you. Headquarters. Said they'll need you Friday. I asked if there was anything else. She just said, "No.""

"Uh, thanks," he said. "Let's get the party started."

"Again?" asked Kristi. "I don't suppose you could tell me what this is about."

"Yes, again," he sighed, "and no, I can't. Sorry."

She watched him walk toward the hangar. She looked at Annie. "He made sure I was safe," she said.

"Yeah," said Annie, "it almost makes me wish I was the one out there."

Eleven

Larry Pritchett approached the door of the OIC's office. She'd sent for him, and he was wary. In his experience, these things never came to any good. Usually a reprimand of some kind. He couldn't think of anything he'd done wrong lately. Well, nothing she knew about anyway. He'd worn a clean and pressed work uniform, shined his shoes, and ensured his gig line – the line of the edge of his shirt, belt buckle, and trouser fly – was straight. It wasn't an inspection, but whatever it was, he didn't want to start by being reprimanded for his appearance.

He was about to knock when the commander looked up and motioned him in. He took a deep breath, opened the door, and stepped into her office.

"Close the door behind you," she said.

He complied, closing the door softly. His hands were shaking. He took measured steps to the square in front of her desk and assumed the position of attention. Smartly, but not rigidly. He didn't want her to think he was afraid. Although –

"Thank you for coming to see me," she started. "I've been looking over some files."

He noted the single file on her desk. It looked like a personnel file, probably his. He didn't know if he should respond, so he didn't.

"I see you have just about two years left on your current enlistment."

"Yes, ma'am."

"I also see that you won't be eligible for reenlistment unless you are promoted."

"No, ma'am. Or, yes, ma'am."

"Your record shows you made some mistakes in your past. Foolish things that don't matter much in the civilian world but are enough to keep you from being promoted in the service."

"Yes, ma'am. You see," he started.

"What you did doesn't matter so much that it may mean the service loses you," she said, cutting him off. "You're coming up on eight years. If you've been in that long, I would think you'd like to stay for retirement. Eight years is a lot to throw away. There are civilian equivalents for a boatswain's mate. I'm sure you could find a decent job, but it would be nice to have a retirement check and medical, in addition." She paused. "Would it be fair to say you'd like to continue? To retirement?"

"Yes, ma'am. It's just," he started. She cut him off with a wave of her hand.

"Well, we should look for ways you can overcome these small lapses of your past."

"Ma'am?" Maybe this could be a good thing.

"We need to find special projects and make sure your evaluations going forward are top-notch. Have a seat," she said, tilting her head to a chair positioned facing the corner of the desk at forty-five degrees.

Pritchett hesitated. *A trap?*

"Go ahead," she said.

He moved slowly and took a seat, sitting at attention.

"You can relax. We're talking about making sure you get what you want. And need."

His position relaxed slightly. He was beginning to feel special. None of the enlisted were permitted to sit in this office since she'd arrived.

"So, this station is like a ship. I, of course, am the captain. If this were like an old Roman ship, the crew would be moving the ship using oars. I'd need a full crew. With everyone pulling their weight. If someone were missing on one side of the ship, it wouldn't be balanced. It would be impossible to keep moving in a straight line. Toward the objective, whatever that was. You understand, don't you?"

"Yes, ma'am," he answered, not understanding at all.

"Good. That's why I don't want to lose you. You're part of the crew that we need to keep everything working. An important part of the crew."

"Thank you, ma'am," he said, still not understanding.

"But, just like a ship, I can't possibly keep track of everything by myself. All the systems and needs of the crew. I have to get information from the crew. Mostly through the chain of command, but also unofficially. To do my job better. You see that, don't you?"

"Yes, ma'am."

"Good. In order to help you – for me to do the things I need to do to get you promoted – I'm going to need some help from you. To help me be more efficient in my job."

"I don't – what help do you need from me, ma'am?" he asked.

"I need to know what is going on in the station. Not the everyday things. Not the things I get in reports. But if somebody does something out of the ordinary. Maybe something that isn't according to regulations," she said.

"Like a spy? Like spying on my coworkers?"

"No, not spying. But things happen that people don't tell me about. Maybe they just don't want me to know. Maybe it's embarrassing. Or against regulations. You know, like almost running out of fuel on a rescue. That helped me out."

He smiled.

"Sometimes, I hear about things from headquarters. That doesn't help me. It doesn't help you. You see. It isn't spying. You're just letting me know about things that will help me make this a better station. So, I won't be embarrassed when someone at headquarters asks me questions. I just want to be able to answer their questions. That seems fair, doesn't it?"

"Yes, ma'am, I guess so."

"Good. Now, the rest of the enlisted personnel might mistake this as spying, like you did until I explained it. And, they might avoid telling you things. So, here is a phone number," she said, handing him a slip of paper. "When you have something you think I should know, something the others might not want me to know about, just leave a message at this number. And, that way, we can just keep this between us. Got it?"

"Uh, yes, ma'am."

"Good. In the meantime, I'm going to see about ways to boost your evaluations, so you can get what you want. That's all for now. And, we can keep this meeting just between us. If anyone asks, we were just going over your file."

Pritchett rose and turned to leave. He turned back. "Thank you, commander. I appreciate this second chance."

A smile crossed her face. "You're welcome. I think it will be a good opportunity for you, and we can help each other."

Pritchett left the office and closed the door, sticking the paper into his pocket. *Maybe I'll have my retirement. And show the others.*

Twelve

The sun was high in the sky, and a light breeze had blown all the smog away. The Coast Guard Cutter San Lorenzo sat tied up at the pier in Long Beach harbor. Kristi was in civilian clothes. Commander Cruise had left a message telling her to come in civvies. The cutter was a good-sized ship, larger than she imagined, and seemed to get larger the closer she got to it. She took a deep breath and started up the gangway. Before she stepped onto the ship, she asked to come aboard.

"Uh, Kristi Swanson. I request permission to come aboard. I have a meeting at noon with the captain."

A second-class petty officer stood on the quarter deck. "One moment, ma'am," he said. She started to correct him, telling him she wasn't a ma'am, but before she could, he stepped a few feet away and consulted with a chief petty officer who picked up a telephone and spoke into it. A red-haired seaman in an impeccable uniform appeared, and the chief approached her.

"Good morning, ma'am. Permission granted," he said. "This is Seaman Mills. He will conduct you to the captain's in-port cabin."

"Uh, thank you," she said, almost apologetic for all the attention. She wondered what would have happened if she'd arrived in uniform.

"This way, ma'am," said the seaman, turning. They entered the ship and ascended a ladder. After a few twists and turns, Mills knocked softly on a door.

"Enter," she heard from the other side.

Mills opened the door and motioned for Kristi to enter. A small bird was flying around in her stomach. She stepped into the room, and Mills closed the door behind her. Her apprehension increased.

The officer she'd known as the OIC at Sandy Bay was sitting behind a table, wearing a khaki uniform and silver oak leaf rank insignias on her collars. She looked up, smiled, stood, and came around to greet her.

"Kristi! Welcome! Did you find the place okay?"

"Uh, yes, ma'am. I'm a little overwhelmed," Kristi answered.

"Overwhelmed?" asked Dee.

"Yeah. The formality. The escort. Kind of the whole thing."

"Annie tells me you are thinking about pursuing a commission. If you stay in the service, and especially if you put boards on those shoulders, this will probably be part of your life. It will become one of the best parts of your life."

"I'm sure. It's kind of overwhelming the first time."

"You'll get used to it. I'm about to have lunch. Will you join me?"

"Sure. Thank you, Ma'am."

"It's the best time for us to talk. They bother me less during lunch," said Dee. The phone attached to the wall behind her rang, and Dee picked it up. "Captain," she said without formality. "Okay. We can go over those items at," Dee looked at a laptop on the table, "sixteen hundred. I've got a time certain at seventeen hundred, so come prepared. Yes. Thank you." She hung up the phone and looked at Kristi. "As I said, they bother me less." Then, "Salad okay?"

"Yes. Of course."

Dee picked up the phone and dialed a number. "George, hi. Can I get two niçoise salads with tuna, please? Uh," she covered the phone and looked at Kristi, "iced tea okay?" Kristi nodded. "And, two iced teas, please. Sure. Anything. Thank you." She hung up and turned back to Kristi. "Lunch should be here momentarily."

Kristi looked around. The cabin was like a small apartment. This table for dining and working, a small seating area with a sofa, armchairs, and flat-screen television. Two doors marked the entrance to the head and sleeping quarters.

"So," said Dee, "welcome to my world. This is the in-port cabin. I use it when we are in port. When we're at sea, I have my at-sea cabin. That one is distinctly smaller. It has a bunk, sink, shower, toilet, and closet for a few uniforms. All in about an eight by ten-foot space just off the bridge. I can't be far from the action at sea, and I get maybe six hours of sleep, mostly in catnaps."

"It sounds grueling," said Kristi.

"It is, but it's also the most exciting thing I can imagine doing."

There was a knock on the door.

"Enter," said Dee.

A coastguardsman entered the cabin carrying a covered tray. He set it at the far end of the table and uncovered it. There were two large salads, iced tea, and slices of chocolate cake on the tray. The man picked up flatware and moved behind the women to set the places before placing the food and drinks. He picked up the tray and started to leave, saying, "Please let me know if there will be anything else you need, captain."

"Thank you, George."

The coastguardsman left, and they started to eat.

"This is delicious," said Kristi.

"Yes," said Dee, "if anything, the food on board is too good. I have to work at it to keep from gaining weight. I have almost no chance to exercise when we're at sea, so I have to do that in port."

"Sounds like you're busy in port, too. When do you get a minute to yourself, much less to exercise?" asked Kristi, taking a bite of her salad.

"Scott helps me. We work out together," she said. "Anyway, Annie tells me you are considering applying for a commission."

"I'm thinking about it. Vince, uh, Chief Ayala tells me I should. I'm not sure. It would be a great career, but it seems like a lot of responsibility. What if I make a mistake? I don't know if I'm ready."

"From what Annie tells me, you'd make a good officer. You're smart, professional, and think things through. And willing to take a risk when you need to."

"You talked with Annie about me?" asked Kristi.

"Of course. Annie's a great judge of character. I do my homework. I remember you from my time at the station, but Annie knows people. You're ready. You just have to decide if that's what you want to do. Because it's a lot of work and dedication – but the rewards are great, too."

"You might be interested in a mapping exercise we did two days ago," said Dee. "We started to map an area about ten miles out a month ago but had to cut it short. Equipment problem halfway through the exercise. We redid it two days ago. It turns out something had changed. There's an anomaly on the top of a sea mount, just about where you rescued those people. I'll send over the coordinates and the scans. It looks like a boat settled in about two hundred feet. If so, it might be the one from your rescue, and it might be possible to see what sank her. I heard about your rescue. Nice work."

"Thank you," said Kristi. She wondered how they might do that.

They finished lunch and started the tour. To Kristi, it was an endless maze of passageways, ladders, and machinery. Dee knew the name of everyone they met. She asked about families and hobbies. She asked about the work the coastguardsmen were doing. Kristi was amazed that it was only two-thirty when they finished. Dee walked her to the quarterdeck. The coastguardsmen came to attention.

Dee picked up the phone and dialed a number. "XO. Captain. Check with the department heads. If we can, let's set the watch at fifteen hundred. It's a nice day. I've got a sixteen hundred. Who's the CDO? Okay. You can head out at fifteen hundred, too. Have a good weekend. Next week will be busy."

Dee hung up and turned to Kristi. "Your future is yours to decide. The service will treat you right. Good opportunities are here if you work for them."

"Thank you. Thank you very much."

Dee started to turn, then turned back. "By the way, Annie has ways of knowing things. Personal things. Trust me." Then, she was gone.

Kristi was left to puzzle that as she turned to the petty officer on duty. "I request permission to leave the ship."

"Permission granted."

Unable to salute because she wasn't in uniform, Kristi gave a slight nod, then turned, stepped onto the gangway, and nodded to the flag at the stern. Despite the encouragement, she didn't know if she had what it would take to be an officer like Commander Cruise.

Thirteen

The sun was setting as Steve Bond and Kaye Christianson walked to the front door of the large English Tudor home. They'd parked on the drive, next to a Mercedes and a Jag. Set back behind a stone privacy wall, to the left of the house, stood a courtyard with a carriage house. Across the back of the courtyard was a four-car garage. Kaye spotted a Bentley parked outside the garage.

"I told you these people were connected," said Steve Bond. "Even if you decide to stay in the Coast Guard, they can be very helpful. They turned me on to a couple of investments that have made me excellent returns. They invest the money for me and deliver my returns. Some kind of a group investment trust. It hasn't failed to bring me an excellent return yet, and it's even easier than using a broker. And, there are some very important local people in the investment group. It's a great group for networking."

She tugged at her little black dress, pulling it into position.

"You're not nervous, are you?" he asked.

"Maybe a little," she said, smoothing the front of her dress. "These people are out of my league," she answered.

"Nonsense. You'll find out. They're normal and down-to-earth. Just rich." He rang the bell. A good-looking curvy woman with light brown hair opened the door. Kaye judged her to be in her mid-forties. She wore a long black one-piece form-fitting sheath with a revealing decolletage and a slit up the left leg to mid-thigh. A two-carat diamond pendant hung around her neck on a platinum chain. Single carat diamond studs were on each ear.

"Steve! I'm so glad you could make it," she said, giving him a hug and a peck on the cheek. "This must be your friend."

"Yes. Susanna, this is Kaye. Kaye Christianson. Kaye, Susanna Stone," he said.

"Well, welcome, Kaye. We're glad you could join us. What a lovely dress."

"Uh, thank you. I'm delighted to meet you. You have a beautiful home."

"Thank you. We'll have to give you the tour later. Please come in and meet the others."

They entered the living room. Two other couples were standing. Each had a glass of champagne. A tall, good-looking man entered the room at the far end. His brown hair had a touch of gray. He smiled immediately when he spotted them.

"Steve! Welcome," he said, striding toward them. "This must be the young lady, excuse me, the officer you told me about. I'm Craig Stone," he said, taking Kaye's hand and shaking it lightly. "I believe you've met my wife, Susanna."

"Yes. Yes, sir. Thank you for inviting me," she said.

"Please, it's Craig. And, we're glad to have you as our guests. It's the least we can do for people who protect our country. You're the commanding officer of a station here, aren't you?"

"Officer in charge, sir, uh Craig. Sandy Bay. I'm in charge, but it isn't a commanding officer position."

"Still, you are in charge of actual operations – rescues, chasing criminals on the high seas, all those exciting and dangerous things."

"Uh, yes, sir," she said, turning red and glancing at Steve. "Mostly, it's routine. Not as exciting as you might think."

"I'm sure you're just being modest. We'd love to hear more about it later. Here, let me get you some champagne." He walked to a highboy, filled two glasses, returned, and handed them the champagne. "I hope prime rib is acceptable." Then, "Susanna, would you be a dear and pick out a wine from the cellar. Something nice."

Susanna turned to leave, then turned back. "Steve, would you give me a hand? We'll need at least three bottles, and I can't manage the wine, the stairs, and these shoes. Kaye will be fine here."

"Uh, sure, no problem, I'm glad to help," he said, setting his glass on the highboy and shrugging his shoulders at Kaye as if to say, 'what can I do?'

Susanna turned, "Craig, would you introduce Kaye around while we get the wine?"

"Certainly. Be happy to."

Steve followed Susanna to the kitchen and a door that opened to a stone stairway leading downward. Susanna flipped a switch, and dim lighting appeared in the stairway.

"The low lighting is designed for the wine," she said. "I'd think our safety would take precedence, but what do I know? Please watch your step."

Seven stone steps led to a landing and a ninety-degree turn to the left. Another seven steps and they were in the wine cellar. All the way down, he was staring at the way her bottom moved in the long skirt she was wearing. When they reached the floor, she turned, looking to find the wine she wanted. It was all he could do to keep his eyes off her breasts. They were, after all, barely contained.

He looked around. The cellar was red brick. It had to be relatively new, but it had the look and feel of an old wine cellar. There were at least two thousand bottles of wine stored in brick aisles.

"Wow!" he said.

"Keeping it stocked is the hard part," she said, "along with keeping track of where everything is. We're planning on computerizing it." She turned and walked down one of the aisles. "Down here, I think. Yes. This way. We wanted it to look like an old-world wine cellar."

He followed her down a corridor lined with wine bottles in cubbies. She paused in front of a group of bottles, looking at the labels. His eyes were studying her body. He didn't care about the wine. The way she looked in the dress excited him, and he imagined how she would look out of it. He was breathing harder, and he was starting to feel tightness in his trousers. He looked away and told himself he had to behave — too much to lose. But lust filled him.

"Yes," she said, "this one, I think. What do you think?" she asked, pointing to the bottles.

"I'm sure your pick will be perfect," he said, leaning close to her, feigning interest in the wine. He inhaled a faint fragrance of her perfume. His heart was pounding. "Besides, you know much more than I do."

She stepped toward him, then kissed him on the lips. At first, he froze. She kissed him again, this time longer. She ran her tongue across his lips. His lips parted, and she pushed her tongue into his mouth.

"I've wanted to do that for some time," she said, breaking contact for a few seconds.

His arms went around her. Her tongue was in his mouth again. Her hands on his chest found his nipples, which she rubbed and then pinched. He jumped from the unexpected stimulation.

"Do you like that?" she asked, kissing him again before he could say anything. He didn't have to answer. Her leg was between his, her thigh pushing against his growing erection.

"I – I," he started.

"Craig is a wonderful provider," she said, "but hardly of any interest in the bedroom. Or the wine cellar, for that matter," she said, smiling. Her hands were pulling at his belt, then the clasp on his trousers. She yanked the zipper open and pulled down his briefs, exposing his rock-hard erection.

"I don't, I mean," he stammered.

"Don't worry. We have a couple of minutes. Unless you want me to stop. Do you want me to stop? Tell me if you want me to stop," she said, her hand gripping his shaft.

"Uh, no. Please, don't stop." He was breathing hard and fast. Was this real?

She pulled the straps on her dress, and the top released her breasts. He was staring at them when she dropped to her knees, opened her mouth, and engulfed his cock. Her tongue licked the tip, then he felt her lips moving back and forth along his shaft. A wave of pressure built quickly in his abdomen, and it took only seconds before it found release. His head curled back, and his stomach tightened. His orgasm exploded inside her mouth, and he began to shake. He held a rack of bottles to keep from collapsing as his knees weakened. She continued to work his cock until he was completely done.

"Okay. Okay. Okay. I'm done. Stop. Please," he said, grabbing the rack behind him to keep from falling.

She stood, her breasts fully exposed and rubbing against him the entire way. "That wasn't so bad, was it?"

"It was wonderful." He was staring at her breasts.

"You like the girls? Go ahead. Give each one a little kiss."

He bent over and kissed each breast carefully.

"There, that's a good boy. Maybe one more."

He complied, kissing and licking each breast longer.

She pulled the straps over her shoulders. Her hand was grasping his now soft cock, squeezing and releasing it. "If you liked that, Craig will be out all-day next Tuesday. Come over about noon. Park inside the privacy wall by the carriage house. Out of sight. It will be more fun than this. I promise." She kissed him and stuck her tongue deep into his mouth. Then, "You'd better put him away. And, we better not forget the wine."

They grabbed three bottles of red wine and headed back up the steps. He was transfixed as he watched her bottom sway the entire time, wondering what Tuesday might bring.

Fourteen

Kristi took a deep breath and entered the OIC's office. Her hands were sweating, and that bird was flying around in her stomach. She needed Lieutenant Commander Christianson's endorsement to submit her application up the chain of command for admission into a commissioning program. It was common knowledge that Christianson thought that as an officer, she was a superior human to those who were enlisted. She'd been heard to say that more than once.

She stepped forward into the little box she hated in front of the OIC's desk. "Petty Officer First Class Swanson reporting, ma'am." Her eyes were locked straight ahead, over the OIC's head, on the wall beyond.

Christianson didn't acknowledge her entrance and continued to look at a file folder she had open in her hand. Thirty seconds later, she looked up and inspected Kristi closely. Head to toe.

Kristi knew nothing was out of place. She'd had McPherson's help in getting ready for this. They'd checked everything three times. Her hair was a little long, but she'd French braided it and pinned it up. That was allowed.

Christianson closed the folder, tossed it onto her desk, and leaned back in her chair. "Well, Swanson, I see you want to apply for a commissioning program."

"Yes, ma'am."

"Commissions are for the elite."

"Yes, ma'am."

"What makes you qualified for this elite status?"

"I've been enlisted in the service for eight years. My record is not only clean, but I also have superior evaluations. I have a variety of experiences," Kristi began.

"Yes, yes. That's all well and good. I'm sure all the other candidates – at least those with prior service – can say pretty much the same. I'm not sure what makes you superior."

Kristi felt her face heat up. She knew this might not be easy, but she didn't think the first officer in her chain of command would be openly hostile.

"I believe I have the qualities needed to be an effective leader," she said.

Christianson leaned forward in her chair and placed her forearms on her desk. A slight smile crossed her face, then faded. "So, tell me what qualities you have that would make you an effective leader."

"As far as management, I allocate human and materiel resources to their most effective use. Even in times of personnel shortage, I have been able to cover all requirements."

"I thought that was Chief Ayala's job."

"Yes, ma'am, he has the final say, but he has delegated much of that to me." Realizing she might have hung Chief Ayala out to dry, she added, "as a matter of training. He is interested in my professional development. He reviews my work and makes changes if and when needed. In addition to those, I have earned the respect and loyalty of the crew. The other enlisted trust my decisions."

Christianson stared at her for a moment.

"I have completed several service correspondence courses and attended leadership courses at headquarters. I was acting senior NCO during Chief Ayala's absence."

"Okay," said the Lieutenant Commander. "But you're going to have to show me you can change your way of thinking – IF you expect to get a commission."

"Ma'am?"

"Right now, you are a part of this crew, this station. These other enlisted personnel are your friends. Well, some of them. You hang out. You have a bond. And, it's an us-against-them kind of a thing. That is, the enlisted hold a united front. Officers might not be the enemy, but they are definitely not a part of your group. If you become an officer, you're going to have to change that attitude. The enlisted personnel can no longer be your friends. Do you understand?"

"I think so, ma'am."

"Good. I'll consider giving you your endorsement," she said, "providing I can see that you deserve it. To get my endorsement, I need you to show me you can do what needs to be done, even if it goes against the values of your enlisted clique. Find out what Ayala is doing and tell me. Nobody else needs to know you're doing this. A good officer makes no excuse, and they don't say that what they are doing is by a senior's order. They execute orders as if they were their own. This is just between you and me. Understand?"

"Yes, ma'am."

"Good. You're dismissed. I expect a report in a few days."

Kristi turned and left the office, carefully closing the office door. There was no need to aggravate the OIC. Her hands were shaking. She waited until she was out of view and wiped them on her trousers. A sharp metallic sound on the other side of the work bay made her jump. Her stomach was churning. Christianson had given her an order. She'd have to spy – yes, spy – on Vince to get the endorsement. She'd never done anything like that. She'd become a traitor. And, if she did and anyone found out, she'd be a pariah. And Vince would hate her, too. It would follow her for the rest of her career.

She walked to the female's locker room. She needed time to think. Even if she decided to do it, how would she find out what Ayala was doing? It seemed nobody knew, and Ayala's operations smacked of secret. And, if they hadn't told the OIC, did they want her to know? She sighed. She wanted that endorsement. To get it, she'd have to get busy. Maybe she could check it out casually. If she could get the information, she could decide whether to tell Christianson. She didn't have to. She wasn't at the point of no return – yet.

She took a deep breath. There were a couple of ways she might be able to do it. She'd start with Annie. Christianson was right about one thing, the enlisted were kind of a club. She didn't trust everyone, but the enlisted had work arounds that the officers either didn't know or didn't use. Maybe those would come in handy. But they'd shut her out of the club if they found out what she was doing. She wondered if betraying the trust everyone had in her was a part of being an officer.

Fifteen

Gravel crunched under the tires as Paul McPherson pulled his pickup truck into the parking lot. He turned off the lights and engine, got out, and looked down the dark road. Kristi slid out of the passenger side and pulled a knit hat from her coat pocket. She put it on her head and started stuffing her hair into it.

"What are you doing?" he asked.

"Making myself less conspicuous. For some reason, guys are always hitting on me. It's gotten to be a real pain."

"For some reason?!" he laughed. "Blonde, beautiful, and an awesome figure. The downside of being gorgeous, I guess."

"Yeah, well, fending them off gets old."

They walked to the entrance of the building, gravel crunching underfoot.

An incandescent bulb lit the black and white painted sign on the building identifying this as the Main Brace. Inside, the smell of cigarette smoke and beer greeted them and the mish-mash sound of multiple conversations. The room was almost at capacity. The long side of an L-shaped bar faced them. At the far end, the bar turned ninety degrees away. Beyond was a small seating area with tables. They walked across the bare wood floor and found two empty stools at the bar nestled between the server station and the wall.

The bartender came over and snapped his head back slightly as a combined greeting and request for their order.

"Beer," said Paul and turned to Kristi.

"What do you have for white wine?" she asked.

"Chard, Pinot Gris, Riesling."

"Pinot Gris."

The bartender moved off.

"So. Why the secrecy?" she asked, looking around the bar. The patrons were divided between commercial seamen and amateur wannabes.

"Just wanted it to be private."

"This is private?" she asked.

"Okay. Away from people I don't want listening in." He was leaning on the bar with both forearms.

"Okay."

The bartender returned with their drinks. Paul threw a twenty on the bar. The bartender picked it up and looked at him. Paul raised his hand off the bar, indicating he didn't need any change. The bartender gave him a tip of the head as a thank you and moved off.

"Two things," he started. "I'm not sure which I should give you first." He turned and faced her and the wall behind.

She stared. Then picked up her wine.

"Okay. First, I saw Pritchett in Christianson's office."

"So?"

"He was sitting down."

"He was what?" she asked, the wine glass stopping halfway to her lips.

"Sitting down. We both know enlisted never sit in her office. Well, not when she's around," he said with a wry smile. "So, something must be going on."

"Pritchett isn't exactly Coast Guardsman of the Year," she said. "She must want something. Something she can't order out of him," she said.

"So, what?" he started.

"Unless he makes second before this enlistment is up, he's not eligible to reenlist."

"Well, I know she's given him some cushy extra duties, the kind that boosts an eval. And he's been trying to pump me for information. He's not very subtle, by the way," said McPherson.

"She wants a spy," she said, "and she's using his evals and possible reenlistment as leverage. Trying to make it all friendly. She must be desperate." She put her hand on her forehead and rubbed. Christianson convinced Pritchett to do the same thing she ordered Kristi to do. She turned away from him. Her heart was pounding. She bit her lip. Inside her was a hollow ache. *This is how everyone will feel about me*, she thought. *Is it worth it?* She turned back and started to speak. Her voice broke, and she paused, "Did they see you? Do they know you saw him sitting down?"

"No," he answered. "I was behind one of the watercraft – pretending I was doing some maintenance."

"You know how to do that?" she asked with a sudden smile.

"I know how to pretend. I've watched Pritchett and some of the others screw around without doing anything so they wouldn't have to go out on the water or do some other work. Anyway, he seemed real happy when he left her office. I guess he can't be trusted anymore," he said. "Not that he ever was. I wonder if she has anyone else spying for her."

"I don't know," she said, staring at her drink. Her mouth was dry. "What was the second thing?"

"Before the swim the other day, I was in the locker room when Vince was getting ready. He had a bandage on his left shoulder."

"And?" she asked.

"Well, you know he wore a t-shirt for the swim."

"Yeah, he doesn't usually do that."

"Well, my guess is he didn't want any questions. Under the shirt was a bandage. On his shoulder. He took off the bandage, and there was a bullet wound underneath."

"A WHAT?!"

"Shush!" he said, looking around the bar.

"Are you sure?"

"Before I came here, I spent a year in Afghanistan patching people up. Anyway, it didn't look like a bad wound – not that there's a good one, but if there is, he got it. Superficial."

"So, where the hell?" she asked.

"I don't know, but Pritchett is trying to pump me for information about the chief and whatever he's doing. My guess is you're next."

Kristi was happy with the relatively dim lighting. She didn't want him to see her turning red. "Thanks," she finally said, "he won't get anything out of me."

"Just wanted you to know."

"I appreciate it."

They sat quietly, sipping their drinks, the crowd around them increasing in size and noise. Kristi looked up. At the far end of the room adjacent to the short part of the bar, she saw someone she thought she recognized. She could only see his back, but as he turned his head slightly, she was sure it was Vince. He was wearing well-worn commercial fishing clothes and sitting with another man dressed similarly.

"Hey, McPherson, isn't that Vince at that back table?"

"Where?"

"Far end of the bar. Second table from the back exit. His back is to us."

He craned his neck, trying to get a look. "Wish he'd turn around."

The second man at the table pushed an envelope across. Before picking it up, the first man turned to look around. He covered the envelope with his hand before sliding it across and off the table. She was sure it was Vince.

"It's him!" she said.

"Yeah. Looks like. I wonder what the – "

"I'm going to find out," she said.

"He may not want you to know."

"There's too much going on. If you said he was shot, I want to know." She got off the stool and started to head through the crowd. The going was slow, and she had to wedge herself between the patrons. One of the men turned. His arm knocked her hat off.

"Why, hello, beautiful," said a rather large and drunk fisherman standing in her way. "Let me buy you a drink."

Shit! "Uh, no, thank you. My, uh, husband is waiting for me over there," she said, pointing at the rear exit.

"Well, he shouldn't leave you alone to wander through the bar by yourself."

85

"Please, sir," said McPherson appearing by her side, "my sister just found out she's pregnant, and she's going to tell her husband the good news."

The stranger eyed them suspiciously, then let them pass.

"Nice. Now I'm pregnant?"

"Hey, I was just trying to help, and if you need anybody to help you out, I'd be willing."

She gave him an icy stare.

"Fine," he said, holding his hands up. "Just wanted to be helpful."

They wound their way through the crowd, but when they reached the table, it was empty. Two mugs remained, each half-filled with beer. Kristi pushed her way to the exit and went out into the dark. An old blue sedan pulled out and sped down the road, throwing gravel as it did.

"Well, shit. What the hell was that all about?"

"You got me," said McPherson. "Whatever it is, it may be connected to those calls he gets from headquarters. I don't know if I want to know."

"Yeah, well, apparent payments. Gunshot wounds. I want to know." She paused. "Oh, and by the way, if anybody at the station finds out about my 'pregnancy,' there'll be hell to pay."

Sixteen

Kristi sat in an overstuffed chair in the station lounge, sipping a cup of tea. It was still early in the day. She was checking the duty roster. McPherson entered and plopped down on the couch.

"Long day?" she asked with a smile.

"Just checking the med boxes and seals," he answered. He looked at the one cupper, trying to decide if moving was worth the effort.

"Anything out of line?"

He turned back. "The seal on the narcotics in the box in boat one was broken. Nothing gone, but having the seal broken isn't good."

"Who's used that boat?" she asked.

"Several people. I've got my suspicions. I shouldn't say anything. I'm not sure."

"But?" she asked.

"I won't say, but if you can guess," he said.

"Pritchett?"

"Well, that didn't take you long. Yeah. Like I said, no proof, but I'll keep an eye on it. I'll start checking them more often than they need to be. He may be trying to see if we are checking them at all and if they aren't, maybe we won't notice any missing drugs. That guy seems to cause more work wherever he goes." He paused. "And if it isn't him, I'll take it all back and apologize. To you."

The phone rang. McPherson picked it up. "Lounge, McPherson." Pause. "Oh, hi! Yup. Want to," Pause. "Okay. I'll let her know." He hung up and looked at her. "Annie. Says if you have a minute could you come by her office."

"Sure." Kristi pulled herself from the chair and headed for Annie's office. The door was open when she arrived, but she knocked anyway.

Annie was concentrating on a newspaper. When she heard the knock, she looked up. "Have you seen this crap?"

"Which crap?" asked Kristi.

"Let me read it to you. Quote, On Friday night, April 28, a rescue craft from Sandy Bay Coast Guard Station saved a family of three from a sinking pleasure craft. The rescue happened during heavy seas caused by a storm blowing in from the northwest. In good health and spirits, the family praised the Coast Guard for their safety. Lieutenant Commander Kaye Christianson, the officer in charge of the station, stated that such rescues are the tradition of the service. Although this one was under hazardous conditions, she is happy that the Sandy Bay station could provide this positive result. When asked about this particular rescue, State Representative Fran Hoenig stated that she was going to recommend the Sandy Bay officer in charge for a commendation."

Kristi was staring at her.

"So," continued Annie, "is there anything or anyone who seems to be missing from that little article?"

"I was just doing my job. It seems like a lot of times, the person in charge gets credit for what station or ship personnel did."

"You've got to be kidding me! This wasn't a station rescue. She was on a boondoggle in another town. She wasn't out in the storm – on the boat. You were! This is bull shit!"

"Well," said Kristi, "there isn't much I can do. I have to get her endorsement on my application, and I can't very well go down to her office and ask what's going on. Just one more reason I want to be the one sitting on my ass doing nothing while getting all the credit."

"You don't mean that," said Annie. "It's just wrong."

"There's nothing I can do."

"That's what makes it such a piece of crap. Probably the work of that snake Bond. This is just the kind of thing he'd do. She gets commended and has essentially nothing to do with it." Annie paused. "Nothing to do with the rescue and even threatened to punish you. There's got to be a way."

"If anything happens, she'll take it out on me. Maybe kill any plans I have."

89

"Maybe there's a way that doesn't circle back to you. I'll think of something," said Annie.

"Well, keep me out of it. I don't want to know. And I don't want anything to land in my lap."

"Don't worry," said Annie. "It will come completely out of left field."

Seventeen

Friday afternoon, Kristi watched as Vince ended a call on his phone and waited for him to get into his car. He backed out of his spot and headed out of the station. She guessed he would drive to headquarters, so she gave him a healthy head start before getting into her car and following. For once, she was glad she had an older and ordinary vehicle. If she had one like his Thunderbird, he'd spot her in a minute.

She followed him to a deserted two-lane, asphalt road that wound around the back of headquarters. She knew nobody was following her, but she kept looking around to check. Her hands were shaking.

She pulled off the road and parked out of view behind a group of trees when he turned to enter the base. He passed through a fortified gate guarded by an armed sentry. She wondered if his assignment was inside and decided to wait to see what happened.

Twenty minutes later, she was about to leave when a small, ten-year-old faded blue four-door sedan approached the gate from inside. She ducked down in the driver's seat. As the car passed, she saw Vince alone in the car, going in the opposite direction. When he was a quarter-mile down the road, she spun her car around and began to follow.

They drove north, the ocean on their left. She stayed as far behind him as she could while still keeping him in view. She didn't want to lose him. Twenty-five minutes later, after rounding a curve, she couldn't see him and sped up, hoping to close the distance. She spotted his car in a service station a minute later and panicked. She passed the station and drove half a mile further to a side road. She pulled in and turned around. She'd wait until he passed, then take up the tail again. She was betraying him and violating his trust to get information to advance her career. But she wanted the respect that came with being an officer, and she was determined to get Christianson's endorsement. She'd get the information and then decide if she would use it. Still, she wondered if this is what officers really did and, if so, whether she wanted to be a member of that club.

The blue car passed, and she started, but before turning onto the highway, a pickup truck with an oversized camper passed. She pulled in behind that vehicle, cursing that she couldn't see his car. She couldn't take a chance on passing the truck in case Ayala was watching in his rear-view mirror.

It was another twenty minutes of nail-biting anxiety before the pickup slowed, then turned into a convenience store lot. Kristi looked around for Ayala's car. Not seeing it, she sped up cautiously, not wanting to repeat her earlier mistake. In a few minutes, she saw him ahead and slowed. He slowed and turned left down a slight incline and into a commercial parking lot filled with semi-trailers. There was a large windowless building sitting on a large wharf. A warehouse of some sort. Nobody seemed to be around.

Ayala continued to an area fenced with chain link and used a key card to open a gate that abutted the building. He drove in, and the gate closed behind him. Once he was out of sight, she entered the main lot and parked between two trailers to hide her car.

Damn! She thought. *Now what?* She considered climbing the fence, but it was at least twelve feet high with concertina wire rolled across the top. She'd never get past that. She could jump into the water and swim around the obstacle, but could she get back out of the water? Maybe not. Besides, the water would be about fifty-five degrees, and she'd be cold and wet for she didn't know how long.

She got out of her car and looked around before she went to scout the gate on foot. It was secure, and she couldn't see any way around it. She was about to give up when a truck approached from inside the fenced area. She scrambled under the nearest trailer hoping the driver wouldn't see her. The driver inserted a keycard into the lock, and the gate clanged open. The truck drove through and up the incline to the road. The gate started to close, but the truck was still at the top of the slope. She saw the driver throw something out of the truck, then a tan, muscled arm leaned on the open window, a cigarette in hand. The truck started and turned right onto the road. As it pulled out, she scampered through the gate, just making it before the gate clattered shut.

She walked slowly along the asphalt road, keeping her back close to the side of the warehouse. On the other side of the road was water. A small bay she assumed was part of a commercial facility. Boats would pull up, load, or unload, and go on their way. She was curious why the place seemed so deserted.

At the end of the warehouse, a wide wharf was stacked with crates stacked in piles. She crept to the first stack and peeked around. Boats of various sizes were tied up to docks sticking out like fingers into the bay. There were commercial fishing vessels and a few pleasure craft. There was no sign of Vince or the blue car.

She inched across the back of the warehouse, using the stacks of crates for concealment. After working her way across the back of the warehouse, she was running out of space. Only two docks remained. The blue car was parked ten feet from the end of the last dock, where three boats were tied up. The closest was a sailboat that looked to be thirty feet or better. The sails were all down and sheathed. It looked like nobody was on board. The second boat was a forty-foot powerboat that also looked completely buttoned down. The third was a Bayliner. Twenty-four, maybe twenty-eight feet. Hard to tell if this one was going out either. She decided to sit and wait to see what, if anything, would happen.

The sun was setting, and it was starting to get dark. And cold. She began to think that she might be stuck here all night. And have to beg her way out in the morning. If Ayala left, she doubted that she could keep up with his car all the way to the gate on foot. Even if she could, he'd spot her quickly. And there was no cover, no place to hide, near the gate. She'd made a mistake by sliding through the gate. Maybe by following him, too.

A cold breeze blew off the bay, and she shivered. She froze when she heard a man whisper in her ear, "So. What's a nice girl like you doing in a place like this?"

Eighteen

Kristi sat shivering on the padded bench seat in the stern of the Bayliner. Vince was at the shore end of the dock, talking on his mobile phone. After he'd caught her, he'd marched her to the boat and told her, "Stay here." He then went off to make his call. She couldn't hear what he was saying, but it looked serious. She thought about running off, but he was blocking the way to the shore. She could jump over the side and swim away. No. She couldn't. Where would she go anyway? If she ran off, he'd just get her at work. She didn't know what he was doing, but she hoped it wasn't anything illegal. He did get calls from headquarters. It was all so strange and secretive. She knew that she should have kept out of whatever he was doing. She regretted her decision to follow him, but it was too late for that now.

He ended the call and walked back to the boat.

"Well, I guess you're coming with me," he said.

"I," she started.

He gave her a cold look. "You have no idea what you may have done. Does anybody else know you followed me?"

"No," she said barely above a whisper. She didn't want to tell him that Lieutenant Commander Christianson had ordered her to find out what he was up to.

"Good. Maybe the damage isn't too bad." He walked to his car and grabbed a long thin case and a sea bag. He dumped them onto the boat and stowed them in the cabin. "No questions. If, and I mean if, they decide to bring you in on this, you'll find out at that time. For now, you've wandered into something you shouldn't have. Understand?"

"Yes." She bit her lip and stared at the deck of the boat.

He prepared the boat to get underway.

"I could get the lines," she said, hoping to bridge the gap between them.

"I've got them," he said coldly. He jumped onto the dock and undid the bow line, then did the same with the stern line before jumping back aboard. He stowed the lines neatly, then went to the wheel. The engine started with a deep rumble. He looked around before heading for the gap in the breakwater, although they were alone on the water.

"You might want to move up here," he said, motioning to the chair opposite his.

She thought about staying where she was, but the air moving over the open area of the boat was cold. She shivered and left the bench seat, took a seat on the chair, glanced at him, then stared out her side of the boat at the water moving by. It was getting dark, and there was little to see. She was tired and alone. A tear ran down her cheek. She wiped it away, hoping he hadn't seen it.

Once out of the small bay, he pressed the throttle, and the boat picked up speed. He flipped on the GPS and a radar screen. He picked up a handheld radio, pressed the talk button, and said, "Twelve Romeo underway."

The radio crackled, "Roger Twelve Romeo. Time to position?"

"About an hour," he said.

They rode in silence. He checked the GPS and compass regularly. Fifty-seven minutes after they'd left the dock, he throttled back, picked up the radio, and said, "Twelve Romeo on station." The radio crackled in response.

"Can I ask?" she began.

"We wait. Maybe for nothing, but our job is to be here just in case. And, no, you can't ask in case of what. If something happens, you'll know. Otherwise, they might tell you later."

"I'm sorry," she said and realized she meant it. "I," she said, then stopped.

He pulled a canvas cover over the cockpit. It wasn't much, but it gave the illusion of being inside.

He let the boat drift. It wasn't long before she started to shiver again. "Sorry," she said, "I didn't think I'd need to dress for cold."

He reached into the seabag and pulled out a blanket. He wrapped it around her. "You'll probably be more comfortable on the bench seat in the stern," he said.

She walked to the back of the rocking boat, sat on the bench, and wrapped the blanket around her.

Vince sat in the captain's chair. After half an hour, he checked the GPS. He turned and looked at her. She was still shivering. He picked up the radio and walked back to the stern. "Almost no current," he said, "shouldn't need to motor about the Pacific. We can just drift. Here." He slid into the seat and reclined, opened his jacket, then pulled her next to him. He wrapped the blanket around both of them.

She lay against his chest, feeling the heat from his body. She stopped shivering for the first time all night.

"How long?" she asked.

"Best guess, three or four hours. Maybe longer. Hard to tell." He paused. "Maybe I should have just put you back outside the gate and had you drive home."

She didn't want to answer. Yes, it probably would have been better, but she wanted to be here now.

"When did you know I was following you?"

"I thought somebody was following me early on, so I stopped at that gas station. That's when I picked you up. I waited for a bit, then paid a guy in a camper to follow me – at a distance and slower than I was so he would block you. He didn't do a very good job. After that, I kind of hoped the fence would keep you out. You turned out to be more resourceful than I imagined."

"Well, thank you for not throwing me over the side." She smiled.

He was quiet. She saw a look on his face she thought was sad.

He threw a cushion on the side, rested his head on the boat, and pulled her to him. She lay half on him, glad for the warmth but happier that whatever had been a barrier between them had diminished. The boat was rocking, and she was comfortable for the first time all night. She closed her eyes and drifted into a cozy dream.

Nineteen

Kristi crinkled her nose and squeezed her eyelids as a puff of cold air brushed her cheek. She was warm, comfortable, and definitely did not want to be disturbed. She opened her eyes the slightest amount possible. It was dark. *Stars. Stars? The boat.* They were on the boat. Her head was resting on his chest, and she could hear and feel his slow rhythmic breathing. Her right leg was over his, and her hand was resting on his chest under the sweatshirt he was wearing. His arm was around her. Her eyes closed again, and she took a deep breath. Then smiled. This was a nice place to be. Even if it would only last until he awoke. The slight rocking of the boat pulled her back toward sleep.

It had been like this for a short time before. Two years? Yes, almost two years ago. He had pursued her, and she was willing. Not that she let him know she was willing. But that was just before Scott Jackson had retired and married the OIC at that time, Dee Cruise. Chief Jackson had been the senior NCO, and Vince Ayala was promoted to chief petty officer. Vince was transferred out for a year. Some special op. All he could tell her was he wouldn't be able to call or write. When that year was up, he chose to return to Sandy Bay and retake the senior NCO spot. But he was now her supervisor. He'd said they had to stop seeing each other for both their careers. She'd cried herself to sleep each night for a week. Annie told her that he hadn't smiled in a month, then rarely. Was the road to success always at the loss of something else? Then, too, the actions of Lieutenant Commander Christianson made her wonder what she really wanted.

She closed her eyes and submerged herself in being next to him, feeling him breathe. She was almost asleep when the radio crackled, "Twelve Romeo." He moved, and her heart sank.

He picked up the radio, pushed the talk button, and said, "Twelve Romeo."

The radio crackled, "No joy. Head for home."

"Roger, Twelve Romeo out."

"We need to head back?" she asked, deflating. She knew the answer.

"Yeah," he said. He checked his watch then said, "In a few minutes. It shouldn't hurt to stay a few more minutes." He slid his arm around her and pulled her close.

She closed her eyes and relaxed against him. She drifted in and out of sleep. His relaxed breathing calmed her. When she thought he was asleep, she kissed him. He responded to her soft kiss. His lips met hers tenderly and lingered for a long moment. Something warm poured through her, and she snuggled even closer.

The eastern horizon was showing a slight hint of light when he stirred. "I guess that few minutes was longer than I thought," he said. "Sorry. I guess I was more tired than I realized. You okay?"

"So, you slept soundly?" she asked.

"Yes. Why?"

"Nothing," she said. *I wonder if he even knows he kissed me*, she thought.

He sat up and stretched, then stood and went to the captain's chair. He looked at the GPS. "I guess we did drift a bit. It will take longer to get back. Maybe two hours."

"That's okay. I don't have anything planned for today," she said. "Besides, it's Saturday. I'm off."

He smiled at her, then started the engine and headed back across the ocean toward the unseen shore.

She joined him, sitting in the chair opposite his. They rode quietly for a while. She looked at him as he was piloting the craft.

"Can I ask you a question?" she asked.

"You mean another one in addition to the one you just asked?"

"Smart ass. Yes."

"Shoot."

"After you made chief, you could have gone pretty much anywhere. Well, within reason, and had a good chance for promotion. Why come back to Sandy Bay? I mean, I like having

103

you there, but career-wise, you'd stand a better chance elsewhere."

He looked at her. "Sure. Maybe. Let me ask you a question. Did you enjoy seeing the stars last night? Being out on the water?"

"Once I decided you weren't going to throw me overboard, yes."

He snorted. "I joined the Coast Guard for a lot of reasons. To stop drugs from coming into our country. To protect the harbors and coast from terrorists. I wanted to do things. I could have gone to a billet that would increase my chances for promotion, but I would have been filling out reports, going to endless meetings, working with people out to stab me in the back so they could make E8 or E9 instead of me. No thanks. I'm where I want to be, doing the things I want to do — known as a guy without ambition. I can get more done here. And, on occasion, I take a boat out and sit in the ocean watching a beautiful sunset or the stars at night. Things the HQ folks don't get to do and maybe don't want to do." He paused. "I've got other reasons too."

"So, do you think it's wrong for me to want to go for a commission?" she asked.

"No. You have your own career and life path to follow. I hope you get everything you want. And that it makes you happy. You deserve that."

She looked out her side of the boat. "You kissed me last night. While you were asleep."

He was silent.

"Does that mean you have feelings? Or is there someone else you mistook me for?"

He looked at her, "There is no one else."

"So, what do we do? Steal out to sea every so often?"

"People would talk. You know how they love to gossip. Even if nothing were going on, the talk would start. Those self-righteous purveyors of political correctness love a good rumor. 'Perception is reality,' they would say. Again, reason enough not to head to a large command and put up with them."

Now, she was silent. Feelings of love for this man were stirring in her, but it could ruin both their careers. She thought she was the only one hurting, but from his comments, he was too. There just wasn't any way through.

"Coming up on the harbor," he said.

"If you could just drop me at my car," she said, "I'll head home."

"Sorry, but my orders are that you are to come with me. We'll get your car later. You have some people who want to see you."

Twenty

Kristi sat on a hard plastic chair inside a windowless twelve-foot by twelve-foot room. The walls had been painted flat white – maybe ten years ago. Scuff marks and at least one gouge in the dry wall were the only decorations. Those, and a four-foot by four-foot mirror in the wall facing her. Small cameras were mounted in the corners. Harsh white light from fluorescent tubes above completed the décor.

Urban American Despair, she thought, but that was the effect they wanted. It was an interrogation room, and they wanted you to feel uncomfortable. Tell them what they want, and you can leave. Maybe.

The table in front of her was bolted to the floor. In the far corner, next to the door, stood a petite red head. She looked young, almost young enough to be a high school cheerleader, but the FBI badge and pistol on her belt told a different story.

When they'd arrived, they separated her from Vince. They were told to empty their pockets. Vince complied immediately. She'd balked. The agent had told her, "By the authority of the admiral commanding the Eleventh Coast Guard District, you are ordered to remain here until released. No personal items are allowed in the interview rooms." She'd thought about exercising her constitutional rights but decided to go along in hopes of not hurting her career. If she still had one.

Vince had looked at her and said, "It's okay."

She emptied her pockets and placed all items into a manilla envelope the agent handed her. She sealed the envelope, and the agent told her to sign across the seal. She signed the flap, and the agent placed clear tape over the flap and her signature.

Vince had been led away by a tall, attractive blond who seemed familiar with him. Too familiar. A flash of anger ran through her. She started to say something but didn't know what, so she kept silent.

That had all been – how long ago? There was no clock in the room. It felt like it had been hours.

She was staring at the table when the door opened, and she snapped her eyes to see who was entering. It was the blond who had led Vince away. Where was he? What had they done with him? A Coast Guard lieutenant followed the blond. Finally, a large, muscular captain entered. There was no mistaking him. Captain Daniel Yarrow, the Executive Officer or XO, cut an impressive figure. Half Samoan, he could easily pass for a Samoan warrior. She started to rise, but Captain Yarrow motioned for her to remain seated.

"You've already met Special Agent Collins," he said, taking a seat across from her and turning toward the red head in the corner before taking a seat opposite Kristi. The petite redhead nodded. "This is Agent Way of the Drug Enforcement Agency."

"Amy Way?" Kristi asked before she could stop herself.

All eyes turned to her. "How did you know Agent Way's first name?" asked Yarrow.

Kristi shifted in her seat. Something in her stomach threatened to come out, and it was suddenly very warm in the room.

"I, uh, heard that Vince, I mean Chief Petty Officer Ayala received calls from someone calling themself Petty Officer Amy Way before he, uh, disappeared."

Yarrow turned his head and looked at Agent Way, "It appears that you've drawn more attention than you thought in your attempt to be cleverly clandestine."

"So," he said, turning back to Kristi, "why did you follow Chief Ayala?"

"Nobody said I shouldn't," she said before she could stop herself.

A smile crossed Agent Collins' face, then disappeared. Yarrow was silent.

"I was worried about him."

"Worried?" asked Yarrow.

"Yes. Petty Officer McPherson, our health services technician, said that Vince – Chief Ayala – had a superficial bullet wound. He said he saw it before our PT swim. He knows what they look like. He served in Afghanistan."

Yarrow turned to Agent Way. "He was SHOT?"

"Just creased, captain. A minor wound. He refused treatment and didn't want it reported," she said.

"Going forward," he said sternly, "if any of my people so much as stub their toe during one of your – activities, I want to know. Understood?"

Agent Way nodded.

"So, how many people are in on this little secret?" he asked Kristi.

"As far as I know, just myself and Petty Officer McPherson." She paused. "But he didn't want to tell me at the station. We went to a bar, The Main Brace. While we were there, I saw, or thought I saw, Chief Ayala at a table with another man – who passed him an envelope."

Yarrow looked at Agent Way. "I've got a sieve at home that doesn't have this many leaks. The envelope?"

"In the evidence locker," she said and shot Kristi a cold look.

He turned back to Kristi. "I almost hate to ask, but why didn't he want to tell you at the station?"

"He saw Petty Officer Pritchett sitting in the OIC's office. Enlisted are never allowed to sit in her office."

"Never?"

"No, sir. She has a little box stenciled on the floor in front of her desk. All enlisted are required to stand at attention in that square. Nobody has ever seen any enlisted personnel stand at ease, much less sit. That's why McPherson thought," she let the thought die out as Yarrow's head dropped and shook.

"Okay. Tell me about last night," he said.

Kristi related what had happened – leaving out the part about being wrapped around Vince. And, of course, the kiss.

Yarrow listened, then said, "Very well. For now, you will forget last night, the conversation with McPherson, and whatever you saw at the bar. None of it happened? Is that clear?"

"Yes, sir."

"If we need your services concerning this in the future, we will let you know." Then, "I need to talk with these people for a minute, then you can go. Chief Ayala can take you to retrieve your vehicle."

Captain Yarrow rose. The lieutenant opened the door, and they left, leaving Kristi alone in the room.

Outside in the hallway, Yarrow asked, "Well?"

"Their stories check," said Agent Way, "although I get the feeling they're both holding something back. Nothing substantive, but I feel like they are leaving something out."

"Collins?"

"They dated for a few months before Ayala became senior NCO. Maybe that's it. Old feelings. They're okay."

"Good," said Yarrow. "Lieutenant. Get to work on Petty Officer Swanson's clearance. Tell McPherson there's something wrong with his pay file. Have him come to disbursing. When he gets there, let me know. I'll talk to him myself. And, I'll call on Lieutenant Commander Christianson and let her know that Chief Ayala is needed for his translation skills. I'll tell her I'm letting her know because we pulled him more than we originally thought necessary. Anything else?"

Everyone was silent.

"Good. With any luck, we've plugged the leaks."

Twenty-one

Kristi and Vince retrieved their personal items without talking and left the building. The building was nondescript. She thought that if important things were done here, it didn't look it. Maybe that was the point. She was surprised it was only eleven in the morning.

They walked to his Thunderbird.

"What? No nondescript blue sedan?" she asked.

"If I parked this car in the boatyard, everybody and their brother would know. The extra stuff I'm assigned to do is not supposed to attract attention." He unlocked the car and got in. She got in the passenger side. It was a warm, sunny day, and he put the top down. "I think there's only one of these in the area, so when people see it, they know who's driving." The engine started with a rumble. "But we can get away with taking it to get your car."

"If it's okay," she said, "I'd like to stop by my place first. Take a shower and change into clean clothes."

"Sure. We've got plenty of time." He pulled out of the parking spot. As he approached the gate, he slowed. The armed sentry looked them over, rolled the barrier into the ground, and let them pass. Vince turned right on the two-lane asphalt road that skirted the back of headquarters and accelerated smoothly. The ocean was on the left as they headed north. The morning fog was burning off.

"You remember where I live?" she asked.

"Yes," he said quietly.

She sat in the car, arm on the door, feeling the wind, happy to be out of that tiny room.

In twenty minutes, they pulled into the lot at her apartment building. He turned off the engine, and she got out. He unbuckled the seatbelt but remained in his seat.

"Don't you want to come in?" she asked.

"I can wait out here. I don't want to," he started.

"Don't be silly. Come on in. You can have a cup of coffee while I do my thing. It'll be better than sitting out here in the hot sun."

He sat for a moment, then left the car, putting up the top before following her.

They walked across the parking lot to her building and up the stairs to her second-floor apartment. She unlocked the door, opened it, and keyed the security code into the alarm system. She turned and smiled at him. "Twenty-nine ninety-five, if you ever need to get in here without me."

He opened his mouth to say something, but nothing came out.

"Cat got your tongue?" She pointed to the kitchen counter. "One cupper is over there. Choice of coffees and teas in the cupboard. Cream in the fridge. Not much has changed since," she left it there. Then, "Just relax. It'll take a few minutes, but I'll rush."

"No need," he said, "take your time. We've got the day, and I don't have any plans." He opened the cupboard and, after a quick glance, picked a k-cup labeled French roast. He dropped it into the coffee maker, checked the water level, slid a stoneware cup with the USCG emblem into the stand, and hit the start button. When the coffee finished, he added a bit of sugar and cream. He turned and walked to the couch. He heard the shower come on and looked to the bedroom door as a reflex. He smiled. She'd left it slightly ajar.

He sat on the couch and looked around. Not much had changed. The furniture hadn't changed. A few small touches had. The security alarm was new. There were good memories here. They'd spent happy times here for the time they'd dated before he became her supervisor. After a few minutes, the sound of the shower ended, but he knew it would take her time to dress and do her hair.

He thought about a night they'd gone to dinner up the coast. She'd taken forever to get ready, and he was afraid they would be late. Then, she'd appeared, wearing a form-fitting red cocktail dress with a halter neck, and matching shoes. Her light blond hair was in corkscrew curls. She'd said, "What do you think?" and he was speechless.

The bedroom door opened, and Kristi emerged. She was lost in a large white terry robe and had a towel wrapped around her head.

"I decided I needed coffee, too," she said. She walked to the coffee maker, pulled a breakfast roast from the cupboard, and dropped it into the machine. "Just yell when it's done," she said, and returned to the bedroom. She left the door ajar.

The coffee finished, and he added the extras. He took the cup and tapped on the bedroom door. An arm and bare shoulder appeared along with her head. "Thanks," she said, took the coffee, and disappeared.

He returned to the couch, sat, and closed his eyes, trying to recall the times they'd had together. It wasn't hard. He thought about her a lot.

Twenty minutes later, she emerged. Blue jeans, a baggy sweatshirt, and her hair in a ponytail. She still had her coffee and plopped down next to him on the couch.

"Sorry. Bored?" she asked.

"No. I'm fine. Just thinking about the old days."

"Yeah. I do that too." She sipped her coffee. "You know, not that I want to stand in the way of your career, but I kinda wish you weren't my senior."

"Yeah, me too."

Kristi set her coffee cup on the coffee table and rolled to him. "Because then, this wouldn't be a problem," she said. She put her arms around his neck and pressed her lips against his.

Her kiss was soft and felt like heaven. He slid his hand around her back and pulled her close as he started to breathe more heavily. Her tongue caressed his lips, and he parted his lips. He rubbed her back, crushed her lips with his, then broke the contact.

"Sorry," she said, "maybe I shouldn't have. I needed to – memories, you know. I wondered if,"

"I liked it very much. If that's any consolation. But,"

"Yeah, I know. Until one of us isn't over or under the other – chain of command, that is,"

"Yeah. Dammit!" he said. "We should go. You look great, by the way."

"It's just,"

"Doesn't matter. You're beautiful in anything you wear." He paused and looked at her again. "We'd better go," he said.

They walked to the door. She reached for the doorknob. He put his arms around her and crushed his lips against hers. Her mouth opened, and he pushed his tongue into hers. Her tongue massaged his. Their bodies pressed together. Her breasts crushed against his chest. One more soft kiss. Then they parted.

"I just needed – you know – to remember," he said.

"Yeah. No problem. Let me know if you need to have your memory jogged again."

"Could be real trouble," he said.

"Yeah." She took a deep breath and opened the door. She reset the alarm and closed and locked the door. He led the way down the stairs. She stumbled, and he caught her.

"Thank you," she said. "I didn't mean,"

"It's okay."

They walked to the car. He opened the door and put the top down, then walked to her side and opened her door. She slid in. He hopped into the driver's seat and started the car. He pulled out of the spot and headed out of the lot.

In a car parked under a tree a hundred feet away, Larry Pritchett reviewed the pictures he'd taken on his mobile phone.

"This ought to help me out," he said, smiling.

Twenty-two

Steve Bond lay naked against the short headboard in the carriage house bedroom. His body was covered in sweat, and the scent of lavender was in the air. He was admiring Susanna's bare bottom as she bent to pour him a glass of champagne. She turned, and he smiled. He didn't care if she caught him. He wanted her to know he was admiring her.

She picked up the flutes, returned, and sat on the side of the bed.

She handed him a glass. "Like what you see? Glad you came?" she asked with a smile. She sipped her champagne.

"Yes, very much. Both," he answered, sipping the champagne. He set the glass on the bedside table and kissed her softly.

"You think you've got one more in you?" she asked, running her hand over his chest.

They'd already had sex three times. He looked at his used and limp penis. It was misshapen and sensitive. He wasn't sure. She'd kept him going longer than he'd thought possible, bringing him to the edge more than once before pulling him back. Then, edging him again. Each orgasm had been more powerful – and draining – than he'd ever had before. Once a night had been the most he'd ever had previously, and nothing like even one of these, but this woman was incredible. Not just her body. Her smile was captivating, and he was lost when he looked into her eyes. Just looking at her was enough to make him acquiesce.

"For you, of course," he said.

She played her hand downward, over his abdomen and to his genitals. He parted his legs to give her greater access and lay his head back. Susanna put her hands on his knees and pushed his legs far apart.

"Put your arms on the headboard," she commanded.

He put his hands over his shoulders and grabbed to edge of the headboard.

"Not like that. All the way out. Spread."

He did as she ordered, looking like DaVinci's drawing of the man spread out inside a circle.

Her fingers circled his scrotum. He jumped and said, "Ooooooo!" It was a mixture of exquisite sensitivity and eroticism. He was completely open to her, a woman he'd only known for a few months. There was a hint of danger if they were caught. Is that what made it so exciting? No, she did things he'd never – and continually surprised him with new things she would do. She massaged his scrotum, causing slight but erotic discomfort. He felt her lips on him. Her teeth scraped him lightly as she took him completely.

He started to respond immediately.

"It's been so long since I've done anything like this," she said, pausing momentarily.

"I don't think I've ever done anything like this," he gasped.

"I want us to continue to see each other," she said.

"So do I," he said, thinking, *once I recover.*

"Craig is a wonderful provider, but all he cares about is business. He doesn't care about my needs. My need for fun. My need for," she began but returned her mouth to him.

He had no answer. She was working her magic.

"I wouldn't want to leave Craig," she said, pausing again. Her hand continued the massage. "I love my lifestyle. I need to live the way I am. You understand, don't you?"

"Yeah," he grunted out.

"Part of his business is entertaining associates, keeping them happy. About once a month, sometimes more often, he takes them out on our boat and throws a party."

"Uh-huh," was all he was able to get out.

"As long as he and his friends are off doing business, we can meet like this. I want that to continue. Don't you?"

"Uh, yes. Yes," he said.

"I wonder if you could do me a little favor then – so we can enjoy each other's company every so often. You wouldn't mind, would you?"

"No. What do you want me to do?"

Her face lowered to his genitals, and he felt the warmth of her mouth on his engorged and sensitive cock. She seemed to know just how much he could endure. It was heavenly. His legs started to tighten, his orgasm threatening. She opened her mouth and lifted his penis. She rubbed his leg with her hand, then licked his scrotum before sucking it into her mouth. He was breathing deeply and erratically. His legs were twitching. She licked his shaft repeatedly, stopping him just short of an orgasm. He was beyond caring what she wanted. Again, she edged him. Then again. She finally allowed him his release, and he was convulsing, no longer conscious of where he was.

She looked at the clock. "Oh, it's getting late. I was having so much fun I lost track of time. Craig will be home in a half-hour or so," she said.

He dressed quickly. She kissed him passionately.

"He'll be out again next week, probably Wednesday. I'll let you know. I can't wait to see you."

He left the carriage house and walked to his car on weak legs. He turned to see her standing in the doorway, completely naked. She blew him a kiss and turned back into the building. He stared at the momentary view he got of her bottom and felt his cock respond slightly. No woman had ever made him feel like this.

He slid into the driver's seat and winced as his trousers pinched his crotch. He couldn't wait to see her again, even though he could barely walk right now. Four orgasms in one afternoon. Four incredible orgasms. Jesus! And, after all, she wasn't asking much, was she?

Twenty-three

Kristi stood on the Sandy Bay dock and peered through her polarized glasses, looking down at Vince, somewhere between six to ten feet underwater, as he held his breath and inspected the structure. She was wearing a single-piece swimsuit covered with a knee-length t-shirt, flip-flops, and a big floppy hat. It was only eleven in the morning, but the day was already warm.

Kristi's watch buzzed on her wrist. A text from Annie. "XO!!"

"XO? What's the executive officer doing here?" she asked herself quietly. She looked around, found a hammer, picked it up, and started striking the dock repeating a series of three beats. Below, Vince stopped, then popped to the surface.

"What's up?" he asked.

"Text from Annie. The XO is here."

"You sure?"

"Either that, or she's sending me hugs and kisses. I like Annie, but it hasn't come to that."

"Okay." He looked to the stairs twenty feet away, then said, "Help me out."

He reached his arms straight up. Kristi crossed her arms and took his hands in hers. He gave a kick, and she pulled him effortlessly from the water. As he left the water, she uncrossed her arms, turning his back to her. He dropped onto the dock in a sitting position. They looked toward the building as a black sedan was pulling in. The car parked, and a large officer stepped out.

"Yup," he said, "hard to miss him."

Captain Yarrow looked around, then headed toward them.

"We in trouble?" she asked Vince.

"I don't think so. Don't worry. If we are, you can run when he starts beating me."

Yarrow approached. "Hello, Vince." He turned to Kristi, "Would you mind, Petty Officer Swanson, if I had a moment or two alone with Chief Ayala?"

"No, sir," she answered and started for the end of the pier.

Yarrow turned back to Vince. "Still doing all this yourself?"

"Gives me something to do. I like doing. Better than sitting in some conference room in a meeting I don't want to attend, feeling the life being sucked out of me."

"Yes, but if you want to get promoted," he started.

"I'm happy where I am, sir. Promotions from here up usually involve some deception, back-stabbing, and meetings that make you wish death would come. You know."

"Yes, I'm all too familiar. Still, it would be a better retirement, and how long can you keep doing the strenuous stuff?"

"With any luck, I'll retire in a few years and do something else."

"With Scott?"

"Maybe. That's one option. He's offered me a position. Maritime security. I'm not quite ready to give up my active life here."

"You could have applied for a commission. You've got a degree. You're an engineer. The service needs engineers."

"Still. I'm happy here. I appreciate your letting me stay."

"No problem," said Yarrow, "you're doing a good job. God knows I'd rather be doing something productive than sitting in committee meetings. I think that's what makes us grow old." He paused. "I've got to talk to Christianson. Give me ten minutes, then you and Petty Officer Swanson come in."

"Yes, sir. It'll give us time to change into a proper uniform."

"Don't worry about that. Besides, I want to see how your OIC reacts when you arrive."

Yarrow shook Vince's hand and then walked slowly toward the building. Kristi joined Vince.

"Well?" she asked.

"Nothing. He wants us to join him in the OIC's office in about ten minutes."

"I'll get changed," she said.

"He wants us the way we are. Not sure why, but I think he wants to see the OIC's reaction."

"I hope that doesn't come around to bite us on the fanny," she said.

Twenty-four

Yarrow entered the large open front of the old hangar. When he approached the OIC's office, he saw she was relaxed and flipping through the pages of a newspaper. He walked to the door and knocked. She looked up and jumped. She quickly closed the paper, folded it, and stuffed it under her desk. Then, she stood at attention and started toward the door.

He opened it and entered. "I hope I didn't interrupt you," he said.

"Uh, no, sir. I was just – surprised. I didn't expect," she started.

I let Annie know I was on my way. Vince and Swanson knew, but Annie didn't let her know. It seems she's irritated the assistant to the point of passive-aggressiveness.

"No problem. I just wanted to stop by," he said. "What's that?" he asked, pointing to the box stenciled in front of her desk.

"Oh, nothing, sir. It was here before I got here."

A lie? He thought. *Why lie? And to me?*

He walked around the office, inspecting casually. The doors to her duty room and bathroom were closed, and he decided not to violate her privacy.

"Could I get you something to drink, sir? Coffee? Tea?"

"Yes. Coffee. Please. Annie knows how I like it."

She picked up her phone and said, "Captain Yarrow is here. Could you bring coffee?" A pause. Christianson looked at him, then added, "please."

Annie appeared almost immediately. Yarrow thought, *Again, she knew I was coming, prepared, but didn't forewarn the OIC.*

Yarrow took his coffee, thanked Annie, then asked her how she was doing before letting her go.

"I just wanted to come by and make sure you understood something that has gotten a bit out of hand," he started.

"Sir?" there was worry in her voice.

"Chief Ayala." He paused and sipped his coffee. "I know there have been questions about the times he has left the station, especially during working hours."

"Well, sir, we were just wondering, I mean, it seems so clandestine, and,"

"It is, I guess," he said, cutting her off. "You see, we have been using Chief Ayala to interpret some things – sensitive things – that we have come across and are still receiving. I can't tell you the nature of these things, but Ayala's language expertise and his top-secret clearance have been invaluable. We thought we'd only need him occasionally, but it has become more than that. I'm sure you understand."

"Yes, sir."

"Good. I've asked both Chief Ayala and Petty Officer Swanson to join us. I just want to make sure everyone is on the same page."

Vince and Kristi approached the office. Kristi had removed her hat, and Vince had donned a t-shirt. Vince knocked on the door. Captain Yarrow didn't wait for Christianson's approval but motioned them in. Kristi headed for the box on the floor.

"Petty Officer Swanson," said Yarrow, "why don't you sit here." He motioned to an empty side chair.

Kristi looked at him, then quickly at Christianson, then at Vince. "Uh, I'm okay, sir."

"Please," said Yarrow. "I hate to have a lady stand when I'm sitting. Unless I'm reprimanding her or something like that."

Kristi took the seat. Her back was straight, and her feet were flat on the floor. She was sitting at attention.

Yarrow took note. "Now then," he started, "I've explained to Lieutenant Commander Christianson the nature of your extra duties. Petty Officer Swanson, you should take note of this, as well."

"Yes, sir," she responded.

"I've explained that we have needed Vince's skills as a translator and that because some of the things were very sensitive, his top-secret clearance has been invaluable. And because of those things, he cannot discuss what he is doing with anyone, including the OIC. I'm including you in this conversation, Petty Officer Swanson, because if you hear of any rumors, you will be able to tell whoever is speculating that the chief is performing sensitive translation services. Is everyone clear on that?'

He received three 'Yes, sirs.'

"Excellent. Now, it's time for me to head for an exciting committee meeting. Have a good day, commander. Would you two walk me to my car?" he asked, looking at Vince and Kristi.

The three of them left the office together. Captain Yarrow said goodbye to Lieutenant Commander Christianson, closed the door, and put his cover on. "That was an instructive meeting," he said. "Okay. You've got your story. Stick to it. Both of you. As I said before," he said, turning to Kristi, "if we need your involvement, we'll let you know. Otherwise, you know and do nothing." Then to Vince, "Always good to see you, Vince. If you change your mind about any of those things we talked about earlier, call me. You've got my private number."

"Yes, sir. Thank you, sir."

Captain Yarrow got into his car and waved as he headed off.

"What other things?" Kristi asked.

"Nothing. He keeps trying to promote me."

"What's wrong with that?" she asked.

"The open billets are far from here—many on the East Coast. I like what I do here, and I don't have any desire to take a billet doing what I don't want to do far away. Besides, I'd have to bury myself in work, and I don't want to do that. I," he let the thought die.

"Far away from here?" she asked, looking at him, "or me? I have no right to ask."

"I enjoyed your close company before becoming the senior NCO, and I enjoy seeing you now. I like what I do, and I like having you near."

"And if I get a commission?" she asked, looking at the ground.

Vince just looked at her.

Twenty-five

Two days later, Lieutenant Commander Christianson was sitting in her office when there was a quiet knock on her door. Lieutenant Commander Bond entered, tossed his hat lightly on her desk, and dropped into a chair set at a forty-five-degree angle.

"So," started Bond. "Did you see our little article in the paper?"

"Yes. That was quite a piece of work. How did you arrange it?" she asked.

"I don't like to give away my trade secrets, but I'll make an exception in this case." He looked around. "You don't happen to have anything to drink, do you?"

"My coffee maker hasn't been working lately. Coffee? Tea?"

"Cola, if you can get one."

"No problem," she said. She pushed a button on the intercom box she had on her desk. "Annie."

"Ma'am?"

"Annie, I have Commander Bond in my office. Would you bring us a couple of colas?" She didn't wait for an answer.

"Now, what were you saying?" she asked.

"Our friends, the Stones. Well, they're not only wealthy and have provided me with investment opportunities, but they're also very well connected." He stopped talking when Annie entered the office with a tray containing two cans of cola, an ice bucket, and two large coffee mugs.

Annie set the tray on the desk. "Best I could do. I couldn't find any glasses." She stared at Steve Bond for a moment before she turned and left.

Bond shrugged, and Kaye rolled her eyes. "Civilians," she said somewhat derisively. They used their hands to put ice into the coffee mugs. After looking for something to wipe the water from their fingers, they each grabbed a tissue. Then, they poured the soda into the mugs.

"As I was saying, they are also very well connected. I happened to run into Susanna," he said and took a sip before continuing. "We were talking, and I brought up the rescue and asked if there was any way we could get some publicity for you. I told you they were great supporters. She asked me about the rescue, and thanks to you letting me read the report, I was able to give her enough information. She has connections with the paper, is a close friend of the editor, and has connections to some state politicians. She told her friend Fran Hoenig, who she convinced to recommend the commendation. It doesn't hurt Fran, either, to get some positive press."

"Well, that's impressive. I've got to hand it to you. Do you see him, Craig Stone, much?"

He took a sip from his mug and looked away for a moment. "Uh, not very much. Sometimes at parties. He may throw one on his boat. We can go together. You have to let them invest some of your money. They're incredible."

"I'm beginning to see the light," she said. "Keep me informed."

"Oh, I also have a couple of other tidbits. Your little blond female enlisted person."

"Swanson?' she asked.

"Yes. It seems somebody has developed an interest in her. She's being looked at for a clearance."

"Secret? Not any big deal."

"No, dear. Top Secret. They didn't want me to see the paperwork, but I peeked. Shouldn't have, but what use is working at headquarters if you can't have a little fun and learn the secrets."

"Top secret? What the hell would she need a top-secret clearance for? She doesn't deal with any TS materials. Hell, even I don't have a top-secret clearance. What's going on?" She leaned on her desk. It rocked slightly.

"What's with the desk?" he asked.

"I don't know. The whole place is falling apart. First, the coffee maker goes out. I have to go to the kitchen or Annie's office until a new one comes in. Then, something happened to my desk. If I didn't know better, I'd think someone was sabotaging things."

"Are you sure they aren't?" he asked.

"They wouldn't have the courage. They can't enter the office unless they stand at attention."

"The box is a nice touch. I'll have to remember it if I'm ever in charge of a station," he said with a smile.

"Anyway," she continued, "I asked Ayala. He said he didn't understand what had happened but said he'd put some shims under the short leg. Then, he got one of those emergency calls and had to head to wherever he goes when he gets those calls."

"Yeah. I still haven't been able to crack what he's been up to."

"The XO told me he's been doing translations of sensitive materials, and they've needed him more than they thought. I'm not supposed to ask any more questions. Made a show of it. I'm not sure that wasn't just a story to keep me from asking."

"Well, I'd still like to know. I may do some further digging. The XO didn't tell me to keep my nose out. Sounds fishy."

She pulled on the desk drawer. It stuck, and she pulled harder. The drawer opened suddenly, and half the contents jumped out. The other half was a jumble inside the drawer.

"Then, there's this," she said. "I tell you, I know it's the same desk. Everything is just falling apart."

At the end of the hangar, Annie sat in her office, a smile on her face. Vince had been happy to help. He'd fixed the intercom so she could listen in on conversations. Vince had shortened one leg of the desk and done something to the desk drawer to make it sticky. The coffee maker had been a piece of cake. Annie made sure to send the requisition for a new one the slowest route available. The first one had been "lost" at headquarters. And Vince staged the call that day. He was out fishing. Steve Bond wasn't the only one with friends and connections.

But the top-secret clearance was a surprise. They didn't just hand them out. What was going on? And who would be able to tell her?

Oh yes, one other thing. Bond had sex recently. Real sex, not some little quicky. The married woman he'd talked about? Maybe. He talked about her a lot. Not so much the husband. Well, that would be nice to find out. It could be trouble for him. Christianson was still on a dry streak.

Twenty-six

Annie and Kristi sat at a small bistro table in a corner of the Harbor View Bar. The window next to their table overlooked the harbor below. A mix of sail and motor yachts sat tied up in their slips. Kristi often wondered how people could spend so much money on a boat and then leave it tied up for all but a couple of weekends a year. Even then, some of the owners hosted parties, and the boats never left the slips. It seemed like a terrible waste.

She turned her attention back inside. The table was covered with a white linen cloth and held two glasses of white wine, water, linen napkins, actual silverware, and a fruit and cheese plate.

"This is nice," said Kristi, looking around at the bar as she ran her index finger around the rim of her wine glass. "We should do this more often."

"Nice, and not terribly expensive," said Annie, "and certainly better than the Main Brace."

"You've been to the Main Brace?" asked Kristi.

"Yeah," she said, leaning back slightly in her chair. "I'd heard about it from some of the crew at the station and wanted to see what it was like. So, I asked Scott Jackson to take me. And he did. Take me to the bar, that is." She smiled weakly.

"You and Chief Jackson?" asked Kristi.

"That was before Lt. Cruise arrived."

"So, were you and Chief Jackson a thing?"

"No," said Annie. "Not that I didn't want to have a thing with him. Or hope for that. Unfortunately, I just didn't seem to click with him. He clicked with her, though."

"You think because she was an officer?" asked Kristi.

"No. It would have clicked with her no matter what." Annie paused and sipped her wine. "You met her," said Annie.

"Yeah. She's smart and incredibly competent."

"She's caring and thoughtful, too," said Annie. "I talked with Scott at the wedding. I asked him what happened. He said it was simple. He fell in love with his boss. He said he fell in love with the little girl inside who deserved love and attention as much as with the strong, competent woman."

"We've all got one of those," said Kristi quietly. "The child within."

Annie looked out the window at nothing in particular. "And, when they did connect," she said.

"What do you mean, 'When they did connect'?" asked Kristi.

Annie turned back. "Uh, it's, uh, - it's just that they really connected."

"She told you?" asked Kristi. "I mean, that would have been court-martial material."

"Uh, no. I just know."

"Know? Know how? When I talked with Commander Cruise, she said something about being careful around you. She said you know things. She didn't elaborate."

Annie sipped her wine, then looked around. "Okay. I've got – let's call it a sixth sense."

"Huh?"

"I can tell if somebody has had sex."

"No."

"Yes. I get a – feeling. The stronger the emotion or more vigorous the sex, the stronger the feeling. A couple married ten years, just going through the motions, weak feeling. Still there. For Dee and Scott, I almost got knocked over."

Kristi just stared.

"I can tell if somebody has been playing solitaire, if you get my drift, or if it's wrong. Like incest, rape, child abuse."

"You're kidding."

"Nope. And – you're on a dry streak. By the way, so is Vince. Just sayin.' The two of you."

Kristi looked out the window, then turned, "And that's how you knew that LCDR Christianson and LCDR Bond weren't," she said.

"Yeah, although it seems like he's gotten lucky recently. Real lucky. Not with her. It might be with some married woman. By the way, why are they working on a top-secret clearance for you?"

"A what?"

"Yeah. I heard it from a little bird," said Annie. "They're working on a top-secret clearance for you up at headquarters. They don't just give those away. What gives?"

"I have no idea," said Kristi. "There's just no reason. Is there somebody I can ask?"

"I wouldn't go stirring a hornet's nest just yet. Let's see what happens. Maybe my info is bad. Happens." She sipped her wine. "So, let's get back to you and Vince."

Kristi's eyes dropped to the table. "What do you mean?"

Annie smiled, "I'd like to play cards with you someday. For real money. I could retire early. I see the way you each secretly look at each other when you think nobody's watching."

"We don't."

"He's looking at you when you're not looking. You're looking at him when he's not looking. You two should be passing notes back and forth during study hall."

"Nothing's going on," Kristi said, looking away.

"Well, I know it hasn't gotten to 'you know.' Cuz' then I'd know for sure. The PT thing was fun. I watched him watch you while you took off your sweats. His eyes were glued to you. And, I noticed he swam just behind you out to the buoy."

"That doesn't mean," Kristi started.

"Puh-leeze."

Kristi was silent and looked at the tablecloth. Heat filled her face.

"We dated a few times before he became the senior NCO. And, my boss. If anything happens now, it would be at least a letter of reprimand, and I could kiss my chances of getting a commission goodbye. My career is important to me. The most important thing to me right now." Kristi paused, looked out the window, then took a sip of wine. "My mom was a teacher. My dad drove a truck. We did okay. One day, my dad just left. Money got tight. Enlisting eased things at home. I want to make it on my own, not depend on a partner. So, you can see why I can't get derailed by an affair, er, relationship that might not even last." She paused and looked out the window. "It would be bad for him, too. Probably a career-ender," she said quietly.

"Well, you guys need to figure something out. I can tell it's driving you both crazy." She sipped her wine. "The sad thing is, only the military would try to define when love is right and wrong. You can't determine who you will fall in love with."

"I need to go powder my nose," said Kristi, and she headed for the ladies' room.

141

Annie sat back and looked out the window. She picked up her wine and sipped. Her sixth sense had grown over the last few years. She could always tell when someone had sex, but now, she could tell when there was a strong mutual attraction. There were auras. Faint, but there. When people were attracted, the auras changed to the same color and merged. Kristi and Vince had auras that turned bright pink when they were around each other. And even across the hangar bay, the auras sought each other out. Whether they admitted it or not, they were in love.

Well, maybe I can help out a little, she thought, smiling

.

Twenty-seven

It was Friday afternoon, and the sun was heading for the horizon. Kristi sat in her car parked next to the San Lorenzo. It had been a strange day. She'd gotten to work early and started putting together the duty roster. Vince was at headquarters attending some meeting of senior NCOs and wouldn't be in until noon. At nine-thirty, she'd been summoned to the OIC's office.

She stood in the little box in front of the OIC's desk. "I don't know what the hell is going on at this command," said Lieutenant Commander Christianson. "First, they start calling for my senior NCO at all hours of the day and night, and now this." She'd been looking at official-looking papers, which she tossed in Kristi's direction. They landed on the desk in front of her. Kristi wasn't sure whether she was supposed to pick them up or wait for more invective.

She was about to speak when Christianson said, "Take those down to Miss Duncan. She'll take care of the details. We'll make do without you somehow." Then, almost to herself, "Not that there's much of a station here anyway." Then to Kristi, "Have you found out anything about what Ayala's doing? I'm not sure it's translations."

"Uh, no, ma'am. I thought the XO," she stopped when Christianson gave her an icy stare. She picked up the papers and walked down to Annie's office, reading on the way that she was temporarily transferred to the San Lorenzo for a period not to exceed two weeks.

"What's this all about?" she asked when she was seated at Annie's desk.

"The San Lorenzo is undergoing a routine inspection," said Annie. "Well, they call it routine because it happens every few years, but there's nothing routine about it. It's a stem to stern, top to bottom inspection of everything. They also test the crew. Whether they know their duties, emergency procedures, all that stuff."

"So why am I being sent there?" asked Kristi.

"The coastguardsman who was collating the departmental reports for the inspection is in a family way and had to go on maternity leave earlier than expected. The San Lorenzo needs someone to collate the paperwork and stuff. Strictly admin. When I saw they were looking for someone, I let them know you might be available."

"But I don't know anything about these inspections. Why me? I'll screw it up."

"No, you won't. Look. You'll have the report instruction. That tells you how it has to be formatted. Each department should already have its information in the correct format. You'll have the last report to go by, as well. The department should have those covered if the last report cited omissions or shortcomings. Your job is to check with each department and make sure the report is complete and collated."

"I don't know."

"It will be fine. You'll see. It'll give you more ammunition for that endorsement. I'd go myself, but this place couldn't run without me, and I'm not sure what it might do to the ship's company if I went up and down all those ladders in a miniskirt," Annie said with a smile. "Now, you don't have to worry about pay or anything, even though it is a transfer of sorts. You might want to take an extra uniform and stuff. You may go out to sea for a day or two."

Kristi's head was spinning.

"Oh, yes, one more thing." Annie had a look of innocence. "While you are assigned to the San Lorenzo, that is your chain of command."

Kristi just stared. "What?"

"Which means you are no longer reporting to Chief Ayala or Lieutenant Commander Christianson. The chief is no longer your boss. He's just another enlisted man at another command. Here," she said, handing Kristi a sheaf of papers. "You have to report by the end of the day today."

Kristi left in a fog. She'd told McPherson what was happening, then she headed for her apartment and picked up an extra uniform. The drive to Long Beach was a blur.

The procedure to check aboard the ship was bewildering. She'd presented her orders to the chief on the quarterdeck, who ordered the second class on duty to enter her arrival into the ship's log. She followed a coastguardsman to admin, where her records were reviewed. The first class told her they were expecting her and she would be attached to admin but working directly with the ship's secretary and the executive officer. He entered her into the ship's watch, quarter, and station bill, then told her she wouldn't be standing any watches. Also, she wouldn't attend the routine training new people usually go through. Unless, he'd added, she received permanent change of station orders to the ship.

When the check-in procedure was completed, she was shown where she would bunk if it became necessary to stay aboard overnight and then taken to see the executive officer, or XO. He'd welcomed her aboard and explained what she'd be doing while she was there. It was almost exactly as Annie had described, and she began to relax, if only a little.

The ship was winding down for the weekend, so the XO told her she might as well start her weekend early and report back at zero seven-thirty on Monday. She'd left the ship and plopped into the driver's seat of her car. She took a deep breath and let it out, thinking how nice getting home would be. Hot bath. Glass of wine. Early to bed.

Then, her phone pinged, indicating she'd received a text message. It was from Annie. 'I hope you had a great day. Vince sends his best. He's looking forward to dinner with you tomorrow night.'

She dialed Annie's number, and when Annie answered, Kristi asked, "What is this dinner tomorrow night?"

"Oh, hi," said Annie. "Yeah. Vince got in about twelve-thirty. He was looking for you, and I told him about your temporary orders. Also, about you not reporting to him for the next two weeks. He just smiled."

Kristi groaned.

"So, then I said it might be nice for you two to have dinner together. And suggested your place tomorrow at seven."

"Oh, God! What did he say?"

"He smiled and said he'd bring wine."

"Do you have any idea what you might have done?" asked Kristi.

"Yup," said Annie spiritedly. "And damn proud of it, too. We'll talk Monday. Have a good weekend."

Twenty-eight

Kristi sat in the center of the couch in her apartment. Her knees were together and her feet apart. She was looking for anything that might be out of place. Her eyes darted to the clock. Six forty-five. Vince was due at seven. Nothing should be out of place, she thought. She'd cleaned the apartment twice. The same number of times she'd brushed her teeth. She'd taken the longest shower of her life and done her hair three times. Then tried on three, no four, different outfits. She'd finally settled on a pair of black wide-leg long pants with a slim high waist and a slight flare. Her top was an oyster long-sleeved satin collared shirt with black studs. She wore black heels, her best, and her best black lace brief and brassiere, just in case things got that far. They wouldn't, but the Coast Guard motto was Always Ready.

She tried to tell herself that it was "just Vince" and "just dinner." After all, they'd dated for a year but never really consummated the relationship. And that was before he'd been her supervisor. It was fun and games to discuss with Annie what it would be like to spend a night with him, but now the chances were real, and her bravado – or was it bravada for a woman – had evaporated. She didn't want to admit, even to herself, that she was trembling. She was assigned to another command, if only temporarily, and the prohibitions were likewise temporarily suspended. It might be "just Vince," but the possibilities were now wide open.

She'd fussed over what to get and make for dinner. She'd finally settled on sand dabs. She'd already breaded them. All she had to do was fry them up. She'd also made up an arugula salad with pieces of various fresh fruit and blue cheese crumbles. She had a baguette and two bottles of champagne. Vince had volunteered to bring a bottle of wine for dinner.

There was a knock on the door, and she jumped, her eyes darting again to the clock. Six fifty-eight. She grabbed her phone, opened the door camera app, and confirmed it was Vince. She took a deep breath and said, "Show time, just relax," then walked to the door and opened it.

"Hi!" he said with a smile. "You look great."

"Thank you. You're right on time." *I'd have chewed the polish off my freshly manicured nails if he'd been ten minutes late.* "Please come in." *Too formal. Stop being formal.*

"You said fish, so I picked up a bottle of dry Riesling." He handed her a bottle of wine, label up like the wine steward might do in a restaurant. "I'm afraid it isn't cold. We can drop it into the fridge for a bit. Give us time to prepare – I can help."

"We'll cool it a bit faster," she said, walking to the kitchen and sliding the bottle into the freezer. "And you could help. I'm not opposed," she said smiling, "but the salads are made, and I just have to cook the fish. Ten minutes tops. I've got some champagne. We can have a glass and chat while we wait for the wine to cool." *Better. Why am I so nervous?*

She opened the refrigerator and pulled out a bottle of champagne. "Would you mind?" she asked, smiling as she handed the bottle to him.

"No problem," he said. He removed the foil and cage before easing the cork from the bottle.

Kristi produced two flutes, which he filled. He handed one to her, then touched his glass to hers. "To a bright future," he said.

"To a bright future," she repeated, wondering just what that might be.

She led him to the couch. "Please sit. We've got a little time." They sat. "So, what's new in the last day or so?"

"Not much. So, what have they got you doing on the ship? And how are you getting along?"

"They have an inspection coming up. The person putting the written report together ended up delivering her baby early, and they needed a body. I'm supposed to look at the last report and the instruction and make sure the "i's" are dotted and the "t's" are crossed. As I finish each department, someone from there will review it with me. I am totally out of my element, and I have no idea why I got tapped." She sipped her champagne. "Everybody has been very nice, but I'll probably get lost whenever I try to find anything."

"Yeah, shipboard can be daunting. You'll get the hang of it."

"Oh, shoot! I'm sorry. Would you like some music?" she asked, starting to get up.

"No. I prefer talking to you," he said, smiling. "Please sit."

Something warmed inside her.

They talked until she determined it was time to start cooking and headed to the kitchen. She got the salads out of the refrigerator and set them on the table. "Would you mind setting the table?" she asked.

"Be happy to," he said. "It's?" he asked, pointing to various drawers.

"Oh, right. Flatware in that drawer," she said, pointing. She put a bit of oil in a pan and turned on the heat. She pulled buttered baguette pieces out of a bag and placed them into the toaster oven. She dropped the fish into the pan when the oil was hot and turned on the vent fan. In eight minutes, the entire meal was ready. She pulled the wine out of the freezer, turned to him, smiled, and said, "Please?"

He pulled the cork and poured the wine. "This looks great," he said.

He held her chair. She smiled. "No need."

"Yes. You are a lady and deserve to be treated like one."

"Until I'm back at the station," she said.

"You'll still be a lady."

"That will be our little secret," she said, smiling.

He sat and lifted his glass. "To the chef."

"May she not kill us both," she laughed. Then he joined her.

They ate leisurely. He complimented her on the meal.

"It wasn't all that hard, really," she started to say.

"It was perfect," he said, "and that isn't easy."

She started to clear the table. "Let me help you," he said.

"I can do these later," she answered.

"Not much of a guest if I leave all the work to you. We can get them done in no time together."

There wasn't much to do. They rinsed the dishes and dropped them into the dishwasher. Vince scrubbed the frying pan. "There," he said. "So, we've got half a bottle of the Riesling and some of the champagne. Why don't we finish the champagne? We can finish the Riesling if we want more, but we don't want the bubbly to go flat."

"Good thinking," she said and pulled the opened champagne out of the refrigerator. She poured it back and forth into the flutes, waiting for the bubbles to subside. She handed him his glass and touched hers to his.

"Perfect meal. Perfect company," he said.

She felt heat rising in her face. As she returned the bottle to the refrigerator, her back was to him, and she undid the second button on her blouse. Her fingers were trembling.

"Um, we can finish that bottle. I've got another one, as well. You don't have to drink any more. I don't want you to get in trouble, a DUI, you know. If you aren't okay to drive, you can stay here."

He looked over the kitchen counter to the living room. "So, is the couch comfortable?" he asked.

"Yes," she answered, "I crash there on occasion, but then, the couch only holds one." Her heart was hammering in her chest. The support from her legs was disappearing. She'd asked. He could say yes or no. She didn't know if she could take the "yes," but the "no" would be crushing.

He looked into her eyes. The wait was killing her.

Twenty-nine

He lifted his full champagne flute and drained it in one swallow. "Well, it looks like I've had too much champagne to get into my car tonight." He set his empty glass on the counter and put his arms around her. He kissed her softly once. Then twice. Then, their mouths closed over each other. His hot breath was on her cheek. Her worries dissolved as the heat of desire grew inside her.

Her heart was pounding harder than ever. He'd said yes. He understood that in staying, they would be sharing a bed. She did too. She'd hoped for a yes. He'd upped the ante. They might not make it to a regular bedtime.

"Um, I guess that's a yes. Do you want to finish the champagne? I hate to have it go to waste."

"Not a problem," he said. He turned to the refrigerator, grabbed the champagne bottle, and drained it. "Problem solved. At least my part. Sorry if that seems a bit abrupt. You can bring yours along if you wish. I have something I've wanted to do for a long time." He picked her up in his arms. She wobbled a bit but was able to hold the flute without spilling. He kissed her deeply, his tongue seeking hers, and she responded.

He headed for the bedroom and touched the cracked door with his foot to open it. He carried her into the bedroom, kicking off his shoes as he approached the bed. He set her down softly, and she set the flute on the nightstand.

His lips hadn't left hers since he picked her up. Now, he was nuzzling her neck, and she tilted her head back to give him more access. Thoughts, emotions, and feelings were all colliding at once. Desire was burning within her. He kissed her neck and began to work his way into her decolletage. When he started to work on one of the studs, she grabbed the sides of the blouse and ripped it open. Little black studs flew everywhere.

"I'll get them later," she said to the man who was lost kissing her chest. She unhooked the black lace bra. Thankful she'd picked one that clasped in the front. Her head jerked back as his lips settled on her left nipple, his hot breath making it rock hard. He sucked it into his mouth and ran his tongue around and across it. Her legs began to have a mind of their own. Her knees started clasping together, then dropping apart, only to start all over again. Her stomach was tightening. Thoughts disappeared. Only feelings and emotions remained. Passion took over. Heat burned. She wanted release, and she didn't. His tongue and mouth were torturing her. Sweet torture. Muscles started to contract on their own. Her head rolled on the pillow. Somewhere she was aware she was digging her fingers into him.

Now, her right nipple became the target. He was sucking, licking – she jumped as he nipped her. He pulled back, and his breath made her nipple even harder. Then, another lick. His

155

hands were at the waist of her slacks. All she could say was, "Hooks, in the back." He rolled her and fumbled with the clasps. She felt the waist loosen. She was pushing the garment down with her hands and feet. He was pulling it off, as well. It finally came loose. The only thing left was the pair of sheer lace briefs she was wearing. She felt him pause for a second. Then, he started sliding the briefs down her legs.

Her primal sense of modesty urged her to pull her legs together. She ignored modesty and slid her legs apart and around him as he pulled his shirt open, exposing his chest. She needed him inside her more than anything in the world. He crawled between her legs. She started to grab him and pull him in hard. But he wasn't moving up. His head dropped between her thighs, and his tongue caressed her outer folds. His tongue was circling where she needed his cock. She started to pull him up, but he wouldn't budge.

"While – I – appreciate – your desire – to make – this last," she gasped, "I have a pretty immediate need." She couldn't say more. She was trying to catch her breath. Heat, pressure, and desire mixed together and built to an intolerable level deep in her core. That mix was growing more insistent with each second and each touch of his. She was hot and frustrated and on the edge. He sucked her inner folds, clitoris, and opening into his mouth. She jumped as he began increasing and decreasing the suction he applied and probing with his tongue at the same time. Licking her clit, then probing her opening. Then, rimming her entrance before licking and probing again.

There was an instant of total clarity and peace, then the heat, desire, and animal need within her burst from her core and shot out to her extremities, then back again, and out again. Waves of energy, relaxation, and tension. In and out. Back and forth. The woman's body she was inhabiting was shaking violently, and there was a growing sensitivity between her legs. The waves of heat and energy slowly dissipated. The sensitivity remained and was growing.

"Okay. Okay. Okay. You can stop. Please. Now," she heard herself say. She took a deep breath and looked down at him. He kissed the inner part of her upper thigh. Both legs quivered. "Uh, I'm going to need a minute," she said.

He pulled himself up next to her and draped his arm over her. "I've wanted to do that for so long. It ended too soon."

"For you maybe," she said. "That was," she started but didn't know how to end the sentence. "God, if and when I get back to the station, I will never see you the same way again."

"I know it isn't right, but I've always wanted to be with you. It will be hard when you come back, but this has been incredible."

She took a deep breath. "I'll show you incredible," she said, "get those pants off." She pulled at his belt while he pulled off his unbuttoned shirt. With his belt undone, she pulled his zipper apart and yanked at his trousers. One leg came off first, and the other followed shortly. She slid her fingers under the sides of his briefs and locked eyes with him as she slowly pulled them off. As soon as his cock cleared the waistband, it sprang up.

"Well," she said, "look what I found. What can we do with this?" She grasped his shaft in her right hand and slowly worked it to the tip, circling the head with her finger. He groaned with desire mixed with pleasure. "Oh, you like that?" she asked. She got a grunt in response. "Maybe this will help," she said as she flicked the tip with her tongue. His back and bottom tightened. She flicked him again and got the same response. She ran her tongue around the tip twice, keeping her eyes on him. His head tilted back, and his breathing became rough and irregular. "Hmmm," she said, "I wonder if we've stumbled onto something. One more thing to try." With that, she opened her mouth and pushed herself slowly down the length of his shaft.

When she pulled back, she tickled him with her tongue. Twice more she engulfed his shaft. She finally pulled her mouth from him and slowly massaged him from base to tip with her hand. She ran her hand to his tip the second time and started to ask if he wanted more, when he erupted. And erupted. White fluid erupted in a quantity she hadn't known possible. It splattered him, her, the sheets, their disrobed clothes, and still, it came. He was bucking like a rodeo bull, and it lasted for at least a minute. Finally, he stopped twitching and spurting.

He was still breathing hard. Finally, he was able to say, "Shit."

"Shit good or shit bad?" she asked.

"You need to ask? Thought I was going to die. Actually, I thought I'd gone to heaven then died there." He looked around. "Uh, sorry. I guess I made a mess."

"Well, we did. I'll be right back." She hopped out of bed and headed for the bathroom. He watched her go. He heard the water running, then she returned with a wash cloth and began wiping him down. "Wouldn't do to have you sticky all night," she said with a smile. When she wiped his genitals, he jumped.

"Sensitive," he said.

"Gotta be done. There." She threw the cloth in the direction of the bathroom. "I hope you don't have any early plans tomorrow," she said, picking up his splattered clothes with two fingers. "Looks like we'll need to do some laundry in the morning." She tossed the clothes off the bed. Then she picked up the champagne flute and offered it to him. He took a small sip and returned the glass to her. She finished it off. "It's early, but if it's okay with you, I'd like to stay right here."

"That is the best idea I can think of," he said, pulling her close to him and wrapping his arms around her. "I was wondering if we might," he started. "Not that I want to presume, but I brought three condoms. I mean, if you are interested, you know, later."

"That's all right, sweetie," she said, kissing him softly, "I've got a dozen in the nightstand. Already out of the box. Ready to go. Just in case." She paused and smiled, then said, "I mean, if you are interested, you know, later."

"A dozen?" he asked.

"Well, I didn't want to presume, and if better came to really better and we got to four," she shrugged. "Three or twelve. Those are your choices."

They both laughed, and he pulled her closer.

Thirty

Vince opened his eyes slowly. It was dark. It took a moment to remember where he was. The naked woman next to him made it easy. They were lying in bed. He was spooning her, with his shaft snuggled against her bottom. He went from deflated to slightly engorged. He started to move away from her, not wanting to wake her, but his movements made her stir. Her bottom wiggled against him, and his stiffness grew, pressing against her soft flesh.

"Your little friend seems to be restless," she said in a sleepy husky voice.

"He's always restless. He's been living like a monk for the last few years. He's excitable. You can't blame him."

"Are you saying this is all my fault?" she asked.

"Well."

Kristi's voice changed slightly, "Your Honor, the defendant claims innocence. Let's look at the facts. He states he just happened to be lying naked in bed behind a similarly naked woman – exhibit one – with his penis – exhibit two – pressed against exhibit one's derriere – exhibit three."

"The defendant would like to draw the court's attention to the cuteness and absolute perfection of the lady's derriere, er, exhibit three," he said.

"The defendant will refrain from trying to influence the court, although your clarification is very much appreciated," she replied.

"In addition," he continued, "exhibit two was irresistibly stimulated by the movement of exhibit three."

"And just how was this alleged stimulation administered?" she asked. "Like this?" She started thrusting her bottom against him.

"Uh, not like that," he gasped as his erection grew.

"Maybe like this?" she asked as her movement changed. She was rubbing up and down against his now rock-hard erection.

"Uh uh," was all he could get out.

"How about this?" she asked as she began to move as she had initially.

His head rolled back. "Yeah. Oh yeah. That's it."

"Your Honor, the prosecution rests. Our evidence is rock hard and clearly stands on its own," she said with a smile, looking over her shoulder at his erection.

"Guilty. I plead guilty and will willingly throw myself on the court's mercy."

"Good. Now, let's see. Punishment. Confined at hard – pardon the expression – labor."

He looked at her.

She gave him a faux peeved look. "Don't worry. I won't pull out the pink fuzzy handcuffs just yet."

"You've got," he started.

"Later. No. We'll just confine the unruly member," she giggled. She opened the nightstand drawer and pulled out the string of condoms. "I hate to break up the set," she said and stripped one package off, then ripped it open.

"How long have you had them?" he asked.

"Two days. Just since Annie invited you to dinner." She pulled out the condom and looked at it. "Now, how do you put these things on? Or is it in?" She was squinting with a pouty face as if trying to figure out an intellectual challenge.

"Um, I think I can," he started to reach for it.

She slapped his hand playfully. "Nope. I have to do this on my own." She set it on the tip of his penis and moved it around as if trying to center it perfectly. She pushed down on it, but it didn't move. She grasped his shaft and pushed again. Again, it didn't unroll. "Maybe it's defective," she said.

"Turn it over," he gasped. "Please!"

"Oh, silly me," she said, giggling and flipping it over. "Who knew?" She slid it down his shaft at a glacial speed.

"Um, you could speed this up? I'm in kind of a hurry."

She stopped unrolling, looked at him with false gravity, and continued to grasp his shaft. "Got a date? Appointment?"

"Please."

"Fine." She unrolled the rest and ran her hand up and down his shaft. He started to sit up, and she pushed him back down. "My way," she said as she straddled him. She leaned forward and kissed him, then settled back and placed the tip of his erection on her opening. Slowly, she settled on him and felt him fill her. When she had him completely engulfed, she exhaled and pushed herself lower. Her head was back, and her eyes closed. She felt him thrust. "Not yet. I just need," she started, and he stopped. She sat on him, reveling in the feeling of him filling her completely. When she was finally ready, she leaned forward, pulling herself almost entirely from him, then she slowly reseated herself, filling her canal again. He thrust. "Be still. I want to do this myself."

He groaned.

She looked at him. He rolled his eyes, then looked at her. And smiled.

For five minutes, she moved slowly. Heat was building, and she was getting close to the edge. She stopped and pulled off him completely.

"What?" he asked.

"We want this to last. Maybe then your friend will rest until dawn." She settled on him again and edged them both. She continued twice more, until she could no longer hold back. She was moving faster, and he began to thrust, lifting her each time he buried himself powerfully. She didn't stop him. Finesse was gone. Animal lust had replaced it. Their bodies moved together in animal unison, and they became increasingly lost in their own randy needs. Each increasingly powerful thrust of his was met by an equally forceful thrust of hers. Grunts, groans, and gasping breath were their only sounds.

Fire burned within her. Pressure filled her and was building. She was holding back, wanting the release to be powerful. Wanting it and not wanting it. Wanting him to push her farther.

Her head jerked backward, and a primal groan came from within her as her stomach contracted and forced the air from her lungs. Control was gone. Her knees pulled together, and her stomach muscles contracted violently. She began shaking and fell forward onto him, then off to his side. She was panting heavily. She was spent, almost too weak to move. Aftershocks remained. She became aware of the man beside her, shaking in his release.

Finally, they were both lying quietly.

"Well, that was interesting," he said, panting. "I thought you were going to kill me there with your restraint."

"It's what the court decided. Besides, I enjoyed it. Didn't you?"

He kissed her.

"Can we get some sleep now?" she asked.

165

"If Little Vince behaves. But I think he's tuckered out. We should be okay."

"I hope," she said, kissing him and rolling over.

He took a deep breath and let it out. Then, he rolled over. In seconds, both were asleep

.

Thirty-one

She left the bedroom and entered the kitchen. She was wearing champagne-colored satin pajamas. The first three buttons on the top were undone, which did little to conceal her breasts, only partly hidden from view. Each time she moved, he watched them sway under the fabric, noting her nipples were hard from the stimulation of the satin.

He turned to look at her and smiled. He wondered if she dressed like this on purpose or just something she did unconsciously. He was wearing his briefs and an oversized pink t-shirt of hers that read "Paris."

"Make you some coffee?" he asked.

"Please. Breakfast roast, I think."

He made the coffee and added cream and sweetener before handing it to her.

"Thank you," she said.

He made himself a cup and leaned against the counter.

"So, I was thinking," she said, "I could run over to your place and pick up a change of clothes. If you trust me, that is." She paused. "It's a cinch you can't go out in that outfit, and your slacks can't be washed. Dry clean only."

"Okay. You're not going to find anything I wouldn't want you to see. I'm pretty boring."

"I wouldn't say that," she said.

"Doesn't matter. Anyway, just grab a pair of jeans, a shirt, and a sweatshirt."

"A set of 'delicates' as well?" she asked, smiling.

He smiled in return.

"I could take your car," she said, lifting one eyebrow.

"Can you drive a stick?" he asked.

"Drove one to distraction last night," she said dead pan.

"I asked for that," he said. "Sure, why not?"

"I'll do breakfast before I go. The fridge is full. What do you want to eat? I probably have it," she said.

He smiled, walked to her, kissed her, and picked her up. He said, "Yes, you do," and carried her to the bedroom.

An hour later, they reemerged. She was wearing jeans and a sweatshirt. He was wearing his briefs and the long t-shirt.

"That will teach me to be more precise in my language," she said. "So, what type of food do you prefer to eat at breakfast?"

"You sound like you didn't enjoy the last hour."

"Oh, yes, but we'll never get anything done, and I'm beginning to think you're going to wear me out. Now. Breakfast."

"Eggs if you have them," he said.

"Benedict?"

"Ooooo. That sounds perfect."

She fixed the eggs, Canadian bacon, and Hollandaise sauce. She toasted English muffins and put it all together. "How is it?" she asked.

"Perfect."

"While you finish those, I'll head to your place. I'd hate to think we'll be trapped here all weekend because you don't have any clothes. Maybe we could drive up the coast. Or into the mountains."

He went to the bedroom and returned with his keys. "Be careful. The car's got more power than you might be used to." He handed them to her.

"I'll try not to break it," she said with a smile.

"One other thing. The dresser in the bedroom. Top left drawer. There's an extra key to my apartment. Put it on your keyring. I'd like for you to have it."

"Even if I can't use it after I return to Sandy Bay?"

"Yes. Even if." He kissed her. "Hurry back."

She reached into her pocket and took out a key. She slid it onto his keyring. "You might as well have one of mine."

Thirty-two

Kristi stood at the table in the conference room on the San Lorenzo, sifting through large stacks of documents before her. She was mildly distracted. Two sets of flower arrangements sat on the side table. The first, a dozen long-stem red roses, arrived for her shortly after returning to the ship. A seaman brought them up from the quarterdeck.

"Uh, for you, Petty Officer Swanson," he'd said.

She started to blush. "Uh, for me?"

"Yup. They were delivered a few minutes ago. The guy that delivered them drove off in an old red convertible. Chief said it was cherry."

She took the roses, set them on the table, and started looking for a card.

"There wasn't a card," he said. "I shouldn't repeat, but the chief said you probably had a hell of a weekend. I don't mean," he started.

Heat filled her face. "No problem. Thank you."

The seaman turned and left.

An hour later, the second set had arrived. It was a good-sized mix of bright flowers. There was a card. She opened it and read. "Saw Vince this morning. WOW. You must be working standing up. Call me. Annie." There was a smiley face below.

Annie! Shit! She'd forgotten to tell Vince to avoid Annie. Not that she believed Annie could tell just by looking, but she didn't think Vince would have said anything.

"So, flowers," she heard behind her. She turned to see Dee Cruise standing in the doorway.

"Uh, yeah, I mean yes, ma'am. The people at the Sandy Bay are wishing me well in my assignment."

"Yes. They must. And they must have gotten their signals crossed. Two sets, you know."

"Um, yeah, yes, ma'am. Seems odd," Kristi answered, trying to look anywhere but at Dee. Her face was getting hot.

Dee walked closer to the flowers. "A dozen red roses. Long stem. Expensive. It seems an odd choice just to wish you well. Was there a card?"

"Uh, no. It must have gotten lost."

"And the others? Any card with those?"

"Yes, ma'am. Annie sent those. For the station."

"Is that what the card read?" asked Dee, smiling.

"I don't remember exactly. Good luck and best wishes, I think. I don't know what I did with the card." She slid her hand into her trouser pocket to be sure the card was still there.

"Red roses. A second bouquet from Annie. I tried to warn you. But then she hasn't seen *you*. She must have seen someone else and guessed the rest. Something I don't want to do."

Kristi stood staring.

"I don't know if you remember bringing me flowers – a dozen long-stemmed red roses – one morning when I was OIC."

Kristi thought back. Yes. She remembered. A dozen roses. No card.

"I can only hope everything works out as well for you as it did for me. I'll give you some time and check back later – sixteen hundred, okay? To see how the work is progressing." She turned to leave, then turned back, "You probably ought to give her a call. Somewhere private. I'm going ashore. I'll tell the XO you'll be using my in-port cabin for a little while. Personal business."

Kristi heard the door click shut. She took a deep breath. She grabbed her mobile phone with a shaking hand. She heard the bell on the quarterdeck ring twice, then the announcement, "San Lorenzo, departing." One more ring. Dee had left the ship. Kristi found her way to the in-port cabin. She knocked on the door. No answer. She opened the door and entered. She felt like a thief in the night. Another deep breath. She looked at her phone, then wondered if the cabin had any recording devices and stuck the phone into her pocket. She could look around. They'd be too well hidden. Besides, they wouldn't record their captain. Would they? She decided she was overthinking. She pulled out her phone and dialed Annie's mobile number.

Annie's bright and happy voice answered the phone after three rings. "Morning, sunshine. How's the girl? Working standing up?"

"How'd you know? Did Vince tell you?" asked Kristi in a low voice.

"Nope. Told you. I have a gift. And, man, did he light up when he came in. Damn near incandescent. Again, problem sitting?" The was a happy lilt to her question.

"Sitting is a minor problem," answered Kristi. "It's peeing that's the major problem."

There was a giggle on the other end.

"He sent roses. A dozen. Long stem. No card."

"Of course, he did," said Annie. "He's a good guy. Just like when Scott and Dee connected. I think you brought those to the office. That was the morning Dee lit up like a Christmas tree."

"But how did you know it was me," started Kristi.

"Really? I mean, REALLY? If it wasn't you, I'd be amazed. Anyway, we need to get together so you can tell me all about it."

"I'm not sure about that."

"Just for my prurient interest, I mean the guy is glowing. What happened?"

"Just because you're a friend. Seven times happened. Eight if you count the first."

"Sweetie, you always count the first, unless it was the vibration of a motorcycle on the way to the party. Something like that." She paused. "Eight? Damn! I'm surprised you aren't in the ER."

"Yeah, well, we have to keep this quiet."

"I'm not going to tell anyone."

"I think Dee, er, Captain Cruise knows."

"Of course, she knows. She knows what, for sure. Who, not so much. But she can probably guess. Roses, no card. She has to know you know who sent them. I suppose you tried to say something about the station sending them."

"Yeah. How'd you know?" asked Kristi.

"It's something you'd do. No station is going to send roses. And without a card. Be glad she's a good egg. I'm amazed he can walk, much less work. He took a boat out."

"Probably going to sleep the day away," said Kristi.

"He'd better do it now," said Annie. "He got a call from Petty Officer Way about an hour ago."

"What?"

"Yeah. He told me he was going to leave early. Had to work tonight. Anyway, enjoy your time on the ship. We've got to get together – if you can work me into your heavy PT schedule." Annie giggled.

"Uh, yeah. Sure. I'm going to give him a call," said Kristi and punched off. She dialed his number. It went to voice mail. "Damn!" He was going back out. It didn't take a rocket scientist to figure out what he was doing. Boat on the water. FBI. DEA. A bullet wound. Superficial or not.

Thirty-three

Kristi was going over notes for her upcoming meeting with Dee. She'd made pretty good progress. One of the most extensive sections of the inspection covered the engineering department. They'd had their report put together completely and sent their senior enlisted man, a chief, to answer any questions. The chief engineer, CHENG, as the enlisted man referred to the chief engineer, wanted an A+. The chief told her that some of her questions could best be answered by touring what he called the main spaces. She didn't want to take the time, but she relented, hoping it might save time.

The engine room was quiet when she entered. Men and women were working on various parts of the machinery. What struck her most was how clean everything was – except for the people working, of course. Uniforms, faces, and hands were all covered with grease.

The chief showed her everything he could and answered all her questions. She was impressed. If everything went this well, she'd be through with her work and back to Sandy Bay in a few days. *Back at Sandy Bay*, she thought. She missed the station, but she'd miss her time with Vince even more.

"Let me introduce you to the CHENG," said the chief, pronouncing it 'chang.'

"I don't want to," she started to say, but the chief headed toward a room with a captain's chair in the center that faced a wall of bewildering gauges, dials, and tubes. The chair was empty.

"This is where we monitor everything we control in the ship," he said. "We're not doing anything now, but when we are underway, someone is in that chair every second to monitor the systems and make sure everything is working properly."

"How do they," she started to ask.

"It takes a while to learn. You have to know the systems. Right now, only three of us can man the command chair. We're training a fourth."

"That means,"

"Long days. And, you can see why none of us have a tan," he said, laughing. He led her to a small office next to the monitoring and control station and tapped on the door. "Here's the petty officer who is putting together the report, lieutenant. I thought you might like to say hello."

A petite brunette wearing dark blue coveralls appeared in the doorway. She held out her hand. "Sandy Johnson," she said. "Welcome aboard. Anything you need?"

"Uh, no, ma'am. Thank you. The report you sent up was complete." She looked around, "And I can't believe how clean this place is. It's spotless."

"I guess this is the first time you've been in an engine room. All of us who work in the main spaces take pride in our charges. I know you're under a time crunch. If you need anything, let us know." The chief led her to the main passageway and told her how to get back to the conference room.

Kristi looked at the clock. Ten minutes to four. She thought she'd be ready. She wanted to be prepared. Dee had been a great OIC. Kristi could tell she had inspired the crew. Kristi didn't want to disappoint her by not being ready.

She turned as the door opened behind her. Dee was standing in the partial opening.

"I'm just about ready. Sixteen hundred?" Kristi asked.

"A small change," said Dee. "We've been asked to help out with a small op. We'll be getting underway shortly. Make sure everything here is secure, then join me on the bridge. Up one level and forward."

Kristi secured everything as best she could. She wedged the flower arrangements with reports. Then she headed to the bridge, "Up one level and forward," she told herself. When she arrived, Dee was sitting in a captain's chair on the left side of the bridge. The person she knew as the executive officer, or XO, was standing at the front center, talking on a ship's phone. He hung the phone in its cradle and turned to Dee.

"Engineering is ready, Captain."

"Very well. Take her out, XO. You have the con," she said. Then to Kristi. "It gets busy up here. Stand right behind my chair."

Kristi slid in behind her, standing in a small space between the back of the chair and the side of the ship.

"Where's our guest?" asked Dee.

"Coming down the pier now," said a voice from behind the chart table.

Kristi looked out the bridge window. A black sedan rolled to a stop. The passenger door opened and a tall, thin blond woman wearing a white blouse and black pantsuit emerged. She poked her head back into the car, then closed the door and headed to the gangway. DEA agent Way.

Dee nodded to the XO, who began calling out commands. "Single up all lines, fore and aft. Cast off the spring lines."

The command was repeated. Kristi saw the gangway being removed.

"Cast off all lines. Port engine back one quarter, starboard engine ahead one quarter."

The ship began to move, and the bow pulled away from the pier. When it was twenty feet away, the XO ordered, "Port engine ahead one quarter."

They moved slowly through the harbor. An officer behind the chart table was working on a map with a protractor and straight edge. He called out an unending series of recommended headings, to which the XO would acknowledge with, "Very well," then order the helmsman to that course. He was also getting information on the depth of water under the keel and radar bearings.

Kristi thought you just took a boat out, you know, point it that way. She didn't realize how complicated the procedure was.

The XO picked up the phone and dialed a number. "Weps, XO. I want the forward fifty readied as soon as we hit open water. We'll test on my command."

Dee wasn't saying anything, but Kristi saw she watched everything closely.

Agent Way appeared on the bridge. She stood behind the XO, who glanced at her for a moment before returning to his duties. She took a pack of cigarettes out of her jacket pocket and began to shake one out. A chief approached her.

"The smoking lamp is out, ma'am. Besides, smoking is not allowed on the bridge."

She looked at him and said, "You're kidding."

"No, ma'am. The smoking lamp is out. There are reasons. You'll be informed when it is lighted."

The agent stuffed the pack back into her jacket. She looked at Kristi, then at Dee. "Shouldn't she be somewhere else?"

Dee looked at the agent and, in a tone so cold it gave Kristi chills, she said, "Agent Way, I know this is a cooperative effort between agencies, but this is my ship, and you will not presume to tell me what I will and will not do."

"Through the breakwater, captain," said the XO.

"Thank you," said Dee, back in a professional tone. "Nice work. Proceed to the coordinates. Let me know when we arrive. I'll be in my cabin. Kristi."

Kristi followed her off the bridge. As they were leaving, someone announced, "The captain is off the bridge."

Then, Kristi heard the XO say, "Course two eight zero degrees all ahead standard. We'll test weapons when we're ten miles out."

They wound their way to her in-port cabin.

"So, how's the report coming," asked Dee nonchalantly.

"On or ahead of schedule, ma'am. Engineering's report was practically flawless." Kristi couldn't believe how Dee could effortlessly flip between subjects and moods.

"Yeah, they're good. I'll hate to lose Lt. Johnson."

"She's leaving?"

"She'll be the XO on her own ship. She's a good officer." She paused. "I suppose you want to know what we're up to."

"Whatever you want to tell me."

"As you can figure out, from that self-righteous woman who came aboard, there is a suspected drug run tonight. We're supposed to help out. We probably won't spot anything, but we'll be ready if we're needed. Coffee?"

"If I may, ma'am, how do you keep it all straight?"

"All?"

"Yes. You've got to worry about whatever this operation is, running the ship, and the inspection. Then, there's the reprimand,"

"Oh, yeah. Agent Way. She thinks she's god's gift. She thinks she will have a say in how the ship is run. That was a pleasure."

Thirty-four

Kristi had just put the cup to her lips when the phone in Dee's cabin rang. Dee grabbed the handset.

"This is the captain," she said. She listened for a moment, hung up, and turned to Kristi. "They've got a development they think we'll want to see."

Dee headed out the door, followed by Kristi. When they reached the bridge, someone announced, "The captain is on the bridge." Agent Way was on the far side, arms folded over her chest.

Kristi slid behind the captain's chair as Dee approached the XO. "What have you got?"

"Big eyes spotted something on the horizon. Says it looked like smoke. Might be a boat or ship on fire."

"Okay. You have the con." She turned and sat in her chair.

The XO turned the ship in the direction provided by the lookout. "Full speed ahead," he ordered.

Dee turned to Kristi, "Questions?"

"Big eyes?"

"Powerful binoculars used by the lookouts."

They cruised silently. As they closed on the target, the lookout reported. "Looks like a small pleasure motor craft. Smoke. We don't see any fire. Nobody observed on board."

"Can you make out what kind of boat?" asked the XO.

"Uh, wait one."

Kristi thought it was a long 'one' to wait.

"Looks like twenty to thirty feet. A Bayliner. A long way out. Looks like bullet holes in the side."

Kristi froze. The bridge was spinning, and her legs were weak. A Bayliner. She leaned over the back of the chair and whispered, "That's – that's the kind of boat Vince used when he went out looking for – whatever he was looking for."

Dee turned and looked at her. "You sure?"

"Positive."

Dee turned back. "The captain has the con. I want small arms forward and starboard. Make ready an inflatable and boarding party for immediate launch on my command. Helm, circle the boat to starboard, one hundred yards, then tighten."

The orders were repeated exactly. Kristi saw men and women armed with semiautomatic rifles and pistols hurrying to the front and right side of the ship.

They drew within a hundred yards, slowed, and then circled the small boat, keeping it on the right. They tightened the circle.

"Lookout reports the vessel appears abandoned," said the XO.

"Launch the inflatable," said Dee. "Careful. Don't take any unnecessary chances."

Within a minute, the inflatable was heading to the other boat. After an agonizing ten minutes, the report came back, "No one on board. It looks like the boat has been shot up."

Something in Kristi's stomach wanted to launch itself onto the bridge.

The radio crackled again. "Looks like they were having a party. We've got a couple of open beers and some whiskey."

Alcohol? Vince wouldn't have any alcohol on the boat. She sighed, and her stomach settled. Still, her hands were trembling.

"Okay, I can't imagine Chief Ayala would be partying during an op. If this isn't his boat, I wonder where he is. Anybody know his call sign?" asked Dee.

"Twelve Romeo," echoed through the bridge as both Kristi and Agent Way said it in unison. Agent Way shot Kristi a dirty look.

"Seems the consensus is Twelve Romeo," said Dee. "See if Sparks can ring him up."

A minute later, "He's about fifteen more miles out. Says he gave chase to a fast boat and lost them."

"Let's head that way," said Dee. "Agent Way can debrief him at sea. XO, you have the con."

The XO gave the course and ordered standard speed. In an hour, they closed on the Bayliner.

"I'll go down – along with Agent Way." Then, as the agent left the bridge, "Kristi, you want to come?"

Kristi fell in behind her, trying not to look too eager. Her heart was pounding.

They climbed down a ladder from the cutter to the pleasure boat. Vince saluted Dee and said, "Welcome aboard, ma'am." A smile lit his face when he saw Kristi.

Dee said, "Kristi's been helping us out, as you know. I thought she'd enjoy a little action, as well. I think she's learned a few things."

Agent Way was all business. Vince described how he'd picked up a fast boat, more outboards than anyone would ever need, and started to follow it. He'd lost it and came upon a boat full of revelers with a Bayliner similar to his. They must have mistaken that boat for this one, shot it up, and disappeared. A second boat picked up the men from the first and took them back to shore. He'd caught sight of the fast boat, but they took off too fast for him to follow.

"Great," said Way, "we lost another one. This isn't going to do my career any good. Maybe we can spot them from the air, but they probably returned and offloaded already."

Dee started for the ladder back to the cutter. She turned. "Vince, good to see you again. We'll have to catch up." Then, "Kristi, why don't you accompany Chief Ayala back? It's late. Take the morning off." Then, she headed back up the ladder.

On the cutter, Dee headed for the bridge. A chief approached the agent and said, "The smoking lamp is now lit. On the fantail." The agent gave him a questioning look. Flipping his head in the direction of the stern, he said, "Back there. The roundy part."

On the bridge, Dee looked at the XO, "Well, let's see how fast you can spin this thing around and head for home. You have the con."

"Aye, aye, captain," he said with a smile. "All ahead full, helm hard over." The engines churned, and the helmsman spun the wheel. The ship picked up speed, turned quickly, and listed sharply. On the fantail, Agent Way was thrown off her feet and landed hard on the safety wires. Her pack of cigarettes flew into the sea.

Thirty-five

Vince turned toward Kristi and stepped toward her as the San Lorenzo spun on its heel.

"So, shall we head back to shore? It's going to take a while. At least you have the morning off."

She took a step back and looked at him. "I had an idea that you were doing something with drug or human trafficking, but I didn't know it was this dangerous."

"Somebody has to do it. I have experience – and enough maturity to keep me from doing something stupid." He laughed. "I guess it's a case of being smart enough to know how to do it and stupid enough to actually do it."

"Well, I worry about you. When they reported that a Bayliner was shot up and on fire," she paused, "I just about lost it."

"Don't worry. I know what I'm doing."

He walked to the helm and settled into the chair. She followed. A cold breeze came off the water, and she shivered. "Sorry, I guess I didn't think I'd be out on the water. I'm not dressed for cold."

"There's a blanket below."

She retrieved it and wrapped it around her. "But you'll be cold," she said.

"I'm used to it," he said.

"Why don't I sit on your lap. We can wrap the blanket around both of us," she said with a smile.

He moved the seat back, "There."

Instead of hopping into his lap facing forward, she straddled his legs, facing him, then wrapped the blanket around his back. She put her head on his shoulder. "Thank you for the flowers. They're beautiful."

"When we get closer to shore, we may have to change positions. It's kind of hard to see like this."

"Yeah," she responded, "but out here, how much is there that we could run into?"

The question settled into the back of his mind, bothering him. But he was enjoying the way she was sitting on his thighs, her legs wrapped around his waist, and her head on his shoulder. He felt a kiss, then two on his neck.

"We probably shouldn't get used to this," he said.

"I know. But I've got the morning off. We can wait until we get back to my place."

There wasn't any more to find out. If she was going to report to LCDR Christianson, she could do it now. Just report and get her endorsement. But should she? Could she? She'd betray him if she did. And one other thing nagged at her. Why didn't they want Christianson to know what he was doing?

Thirty-six

It was Wednesday morning. Kristi's time on the San Lorenzo had ended, and she was back at Sandy Bay, reviewing the station's onboarding procedures for new reports. The sun was up, and the light fog on the coast was already clearing. Two new personnel, a seaman and a petty officer third class, were reporting this morning. The files sent over showed them to be good performers. William Wright was from Milwaukie, and Robert Brown was from Chicago. Kristi wanted to be sure to get them started right. She knew that tours of duty and careers had been made or broken by good or poor onboarding of junior personnel.

She also had to sign off on maintenance performed yesterday. Part of her job had become inspection and approval of work done on the station's watercraft. There were two to inspect today before they could be returned to service. Petty Officer Pritchett had done the maintenance on one of them. He'd had problems performing maintenance properly in the past, and she didn't want anything going wrong when a boat was out on the ocean. She looked at her watch. Seven o'clock. Time for muster.

She saw Vince at the far end of the station pier and headed out the large entry of the old hangar. Lieutenant Commander Christianson was entering from the parking area.

Kristi saluted smartly, "Good morning, ma'am."

The OIC ignored the salute. "My office."

Kristi thought about holding the salute until the OIC recognized and returned it but realized it would only cause anger on the part of the irritated senior. She followed the OIC into her office and stood at attention in the small box in front of the desk. She remained silent.

"Well?" asked Christianson.

"Ma'am?" she asked in return.

"I understand Chief Ayala got a call and left for whatever he does. Do you have anything to report?"

"Uh, yes, ma'am, he did get a call. When he left, I followed him at a discrete distance. He drove to the back of the headquarters property. There's a two-lane asphalt road that circles back there. It's some distance from the main buildings. Looks like warehouses, maybe." The truth was she'd left to follow him, but he'd stopped on the road, flagged her down, and told her just to go home. Kristi wasn't supposed to know what Vince was doing despite being on the San Lorenzo a week before.

Christianson looked irritated and made a circling motion with her hand, indicating Kristi should speed up the information.

193

"He entered a barricaded gate manned by an armed guard. He showed his ID or pass and was allowed to enter. I didn't want to let him or anyone else know I was following him, so I parked and waited outside. When he didn't return in over an hour, I left." She wondered if Christianson knew more than she was letting on.

"And he didn't come out?"

"Not while I was there, ma'am," she lied. She felt like she was betraying Vince by telling her what she had. She'd been ordered not to say anything to anyone. Did that include her immediate supervising officer? And she did want the OIC's endorsement on her application. Birds flew in her stomach. She hoped her pounding heart wouldn't give her away.

Christianson stared at her for a minute. Kristi was wondering if the OIC could tell she was lying. Maybe somebody saw her, or them together.

"Very well," she said finally. "Keep me informed if you see or hear anything else. And, let me know if he gets any more calls."

Kristi turned to leave.

"Remember, you've got a lot riding on this."

"Yes, ma'am," said Kristi with a strained voice. She turned and left. Her heart was pounding. What if Vince had told her about what had happened. Would he? No. But she wondered. She was lying to almost everyone.

Vince walked up. "Ready for muster?" he asked.

"Uh, yeah," she said.

"What did the OIC want?" he asked.

"Nothing. Nothing, really. It had to do with the two new people we're getting today."

"Okay. I guess you were closer to her office than I was. Anyway, you ready for them?"

"Yes," she said, sighing in relief. "I've got their schedule for the day all worked out."

"Good. Let me take a look so I know your plan."

She handed him the clipboard with the schedule.

"Looks good. Very thorough. Good job," he said, handing the clipboard back. "Now, let's make sure everyone is here, and we'll get the day underway."

She followed him outside to the area where muster was held when the weather was good. The small detachment was forming ranks. A heavy dark weight descended on Kristi. Although she hadn't told the truth to the OIC, she hadn't been loyal to Vince either. She was alone and wasn't sure just what was right. Betray Vince so she could get what she wanted? Violate a direct order? Give up what she wanted?

Thirty-seven

Kristi looked at her watch. Three forty-five. The day had gone well. The two new coastguardsmen were bright, attentive, and professional. She thought they would get along well with the station personnel. While they were filling out paperwork, she'd been able to check on the maintenance done the day before. It had been done correctly, and she'd signed off on returning the watercraft to service. She was looking forward to a nice quiet evening at home.

She was standing at the hangar entrance shaded from the sun when she heard a cell phone ring.

"Ayala." It was Vince, apparently just outside the hangar and out of view but not earshot.

"Good," he said, then paused to listen. "What's the name?" he asked. "And where?"

Kristi slid a little farther into the shade. She looked over her shoulder to be sure no one was watching her.

"Okay. I'll take a look. Do you have a date?" he asked. "Well, I'll check it out. Don't worry. I'll be careful."

He ended the call. Kristi stepped out of the shade and walked out of the hangar toward him.

"Oh, hi. I'm glad I ran into you. I want to give you a quick report on the two new people."

"Fine," he said. "Why don't we do it over coffee?"

They went to the lounge and reviewed the report. "Nice job," he said. "Looking forward to a quiet night?"

"Sure. Why?"

"I just wondered. You've earned one."

"Oh. Well, I may end up going out for dinner. A few drinks. You know. I'm not sure yet," she said, hedging.

"Anything special?" he asked.

"No. Just me and, uh, Annie. I thought we'd get in some girl time. You know."

"Yeah. Good. Just be careful. Take a cab if you need to," he said, then headed toward his office.

She worked in the operations office until the watch was set. Vince was still in his small office, so she pulled her car to the end of the parking area and lay down to see what would happen. She hadn't made up her mind about telling the OIC. Maybe she wanted more information. No. She was stalling.

The sun set, and it was after dark. Kristi was still hunkered down in her car, waiting for Vince to leave. She'd asked Annie to say they'd gone to dinner and taken Annie's car so it wouldn't seem odd for her car to be in the parking area. She had promised Annie she'd tell her what it was about later. But if she followed him and he caught her, he would know she was lying immediately, and he probably wouldn't forgive her.

She watched him take a carry-all bag from the hangar and drop it into the passenger seat. He got into his car, started it, and pulled out of the parking lot. Kristi let him get as far as she dared before she began to follow. She'd been caught before and didn't want to make the same mistake.

He headed down the coast. There were a few curves, and Kristi decided to cut her lights from time to time as she rounded them to create the impression that different cars were entering and leaving the road. At the end of forty minutes, she saw him turn right onto a small road. She decided to drive past and then turn around to remain unseen. When she returned, she saw the road led to a small parking area at the back of a marina. Trees lined the right side. She turned off her lights and slowly drove down the road. She was having trouble seeing because there were no lights on this small access road, and it was dark. She finally spotted his car parked on the side of the road. He was retrieving the bag. She pulled in behind a car parked fifty yards behind his just as he turned to look around.

She waited for him to walk in the direction of the marina before getting out of her car to follow. She opened the door, and the dome light came on. She slapped her hand over it and cursed. On this dark road, it was a beacon. She waited to be sure he was out of view before removing her hand and leaving the car. She would have to hide beside her car until he left before she could reenter hers. Otherwise, the dome light would give her away.

The road ended where a fence blocked access to the marina. She crept from tree to tree until she was about fifty feet from him. She couldn't chance getting closer. He was silhouetted by lights from the marina and was removing his clothes. He reached into the bag and pulled out a wetsuit, which he donned quickly. He pulled out a mask, fins, and flashlight. There was something else that she couldn't quite make out. He walked to a small area outside the fence, slid down the bank and into the water. He swam away slowly and quietly.

Kristi looked at her watch. Eleven forty-eight. What the hell was he doing? She could, and maybe she should, leave now. After all, if she stayed, all she would see was Vince coming out of the water, redressing, and leaving. Her chances of being caught were much greater if she stayed. But she wanted to stay. Maybe he would come back with something she would want to see. Maybe she didn't want to know. Down deep, she knew she wanted to make sure he got back safely. Not that there was anything she could do if he simply never came back. But she knew she couldn't leave. On the day of the PT test, he'd made sure she was safe after he'd spotted the shark. Was she being as loyal to him as he'd been to her?

She saw movement where he'd entered the water. He emerged halfway, looked around, then left the water and came up the bank on all fours. He walked to the bag and started to strip off the wetsuit. He was safe. She crept back to her car, careful not to step on anything that would make noise. She hid on the passenger side until she saw him drive past. Then, she got into her car and turned around. She decided to wait ten minutes, in case he'd stopped to see if he'd been followed, then she drove away.

Thirty-eight

Kristi rolled in her bed and kicked her covers off. She looked at the clock. Six-thirty. She hadn't slept well. She hadn't slept well since Lieutenant Commander Christianson had ordered her to spy on Vince. That's what it was. Spying. And on someone who trusted her.

She rolled out of bed and headed for the bathroom. She showered, brushed her teeth, and put on her makeup. Breakfast was two hard-boiled eggs, toast, and coffee. It was Sunday, and she hadn't planned anything for the day. She was in one of those moods where she desperately wanted to do *something,* but nothing interested her. She decided to head for the station. McPherson was on duty. She could talk with him.

She dressed in jeans and a sweatshirt and left her apartment. The day was cloudy, and there was a breeze off the ocean. A storm? She hadn't heard about one. That didn't necessarily mean anything. Storms blew up all the time, but there should have been a warning from the weather service and Coast Guard district headquarters. Everybody off for the weekend, maybe.

She got into her car and drove to Sandy Bay. At seven-thirty on a Sunday morning, the roads were empty. Typical

Southern California, she thought. A few clouds in the sky, and everybody heads for cover. Skies have to be blue, or people think it's the end of the world. Well, that just might mean a quiet day for the station. Few people would be taking their boats out – just a few hardy souls who liked to sail in stormy weather.

She parked her car next to the building. The large hangar door had been closed. Access was through a pedestrian door set into the larger one. She entered the hangar and walked to the operations room. McPherson was sitting in the room, leaning back, reading a sailing magazine.

"Good morning," she said.

McPherson sat up and closed the magazine. "What are you doing here?" he asked. "You're not on the duty roster."

"Yeah. I felt like doing something, but I didn't know what."

"If I felt like doing something and didn't know what, I'd make a list. Maybe have a beer while I was doing it. Coming in here on my day off wouldn't make the cut. But I'm happy for the company. Coffee?"

"Yeah, sure. Why'd you close the hangar doors?"

"I thought it might rain. I've got two rescue craft outside, so I didn't have to worry about taking any boats out of here, and I didn't want to have to clean up any water inside."

"Who's on with you?" she asked.

McPherson handed her the duty roster clip board. Kristi studied it and handed it back.

"Where are they?"

"In the lounge, breaking in the two new reports."

"Okay." She turned at the sound of footfalls in the hangar bay and stepped out of the operations office. McPherson followed her as she spotted Vince walking through the bay. He was wearing his working uniform.

"If I'd known everybody was coming in, I'd stayed home. Cuz I've got better things to do," said McPherson.

Vince looked up. When he saw Kristi, he smiled. "What are you doing here?"

"Nothin' better to do," she said.

"Nothing better than this?" he asked.

"What can I say. But what are you doing here?"

"Uh, I just needed to stop by to pick up a couple of things."

"In uniform?" she asked.

"Laundry day," he said.

"Please."

"Fine. I'm going out this afternoon, and I thought I'd wear these in case I got a call while I was out."

McPherson turned and headed back into operations.

"I'm not doing anything," she said. "I could go with you."

He looked at her. "I hadn't planned," he started.

"Something special?" she asked.

"Yeah," he said, looking around. "Something special. You're not supposed to know."

"The Bayliner?"

"Yes."

"I could come along. It's my day off."

"You're not supposed to know about it. Besides, there's a report of a shipment of drugs coming up from Mexico. It could be dangerous."

"And you're going to run the boat and do everything else. You're going to need somebody to help," she said.

He thought for a moment. "Okay. It could be trouble. Out there and back here. You sure?"

"Yes."

"Remember, I tried. Grab a work uniform," he said.

Five minutes later, they were headed up the coast in the nondescript blue sedan he'd used before.

"The boat in question is headed back from Mexico. Sometimes, they use a scout boat ahead of the one with the drugs. If they see a Coast Guard or DEA boat, they'll radio the drug boat and have it change course or dump the contraband as a last resort."

"So, the Bayliner."

"Right. And we'll be wearing civilian coats over our uniforms if they're using binoculars. If we spot the boat we want to search, we'll dump the civies and board in uniform."

"So, what do you want me to do?" she asked.

"Once we get to the area assigned, I'll have you at the helm."

They pulled into the commercial marina and drove around the warehouse. After parking, Vince carried a bag and a gun case to the Bayliner. He loaded both onboard, then turned to her, "Last chance to turn around."

"No way," she said and jumped aboard.

Vince started the engine as she cast off. He turned the boat and headed out of the small bay. "It'll take about an hour to get to our area." Then, he picked up the microphone, pushed the PTT button, and reported, "Twelve Romeo underway."

Thirty-nine

They'd been in position for almost three hours when the radio crackled. "Twelve Romeo, we've got the likely coming your way. Seventy-foot Hatteras motor yacht. It should be relatively easy to spot. Stop it if you can. Don't take any unnecessary chances."

"Roger. We'll let you know," said Vince. He turned to her. "Looks like you might get your chance."

Those birds were flying in her stomach again. Her hands were shaking, and her legs were a little weak. "So, what do you want me to do?"

"I'll tell you as we go along. If it looks like it's going to be real trouble, we'll wait for backup." He reached into his bag, pulled out a Kevlar vest, and tossed it to her. "Put it on."

"Where's yours?" she asked.

"Put it on," he repeated. "That's an order."

She put on the vest, then put a civilian jacket over it.

It wasn't long before they saw the large boat approaching on gray seas. Vince lifted a bullhorn when they were within one hundred yards and running parallel to the larger boat's port side.

"This is the United States Coast Guard. Heave to and prepare to be boarded."

For a few seconds, nothing. Then, gunshots and small white geysers rose where the bullets hit the water short of their position.

Kristi's head snapped toward the other boat. Her heart hammered in her chest. Her legs were shaking. She looked around to see where she could hide, then looked at Vince. "Are they?" she started.

"I don't have to put up with this crap," he said, throwing open the gun case on the deck. He pulled out an assault rifle.

"Pull a little closer," he yelled, "and balls to the wall."

"Closer?" she asked.

"Yeah, and faster. Parallel to them. The guy's a crappy shot."

She hit the throttle, and the little boat took off so fast the bow lifted out of the water. She struggled to keep on her feet as the Bayliner slapped the waves. She stole a quick look at him. He was holding on to a support with one hand, apparently without any problem.

They pulled within fifty yards, and she turned the boat parallel to the larger one.

He raised the bullhorn once more. "This is the United States Coast Guard. Heave to and prepare to be boarded." He dropped the bullhorn and steadied the rifle before firing at least a dozen shots across their bow. He grabbed the bullhorn and said, "This is the United States Coast Guard. The next shots will be through your engines. Heave to."

The larger ship slowed.

He dropped his civilian jacket and motioned for her to do the same. "We could wait here for the others to arrive or go ahead and board. Boarding could be more fun," he said, "but we could also get shot."

She wanted to throw up, but she didn't want him to know she was scared. "What – whatever, uh, you think best."

"This one is your decision. You want to be an officer. You'll have to make life and death decisions. I want you to get used to making them. What's your order?"

She didn't want to make the decision. If they went on board and there was resistance, they could be killed. On the other hand, waiting, playing it safe, would give those on the boat time to get rid of the suspected contraband.

"Shit. Let's g-go," she said.

"Good girl – uh, ma'am," he said with a smile. He dropped the partially used magazine from the gun and inserted a new one. "Make sure that pistol has one chambered. I'll go first and tell you when to come aboard. Remember, I'm your only friend here." He smiled and added, "Try not to shoot me."

She maneuvered next to the cabin cruiser. When they bumped, he grabbed a line attached to the small boat, and then he jumped aboard. He looked around. Four civilians were gaping at him. He flicked the line around the railing.

"Where's the captain?" he asked.

"Right here," said a man exiting the cabin. "Just what the hell do you think you're doing?"

"This boat is suspected of carrying contraband from Mexico. Assemble all people on the boat here." He motioned to Kristi to join him. She crawled aboard and drew her pistol. He motioned to her to take up a position across from his.

"Where is the gun that fired on us?"

"We thought you were pirates. You can't hold that against us." said the man identified as the captain. "That's not exactly Coast Guard equipment you were riding in. And, anybody could say they were with the Coast Guard."

"The gun."

"Juan! Bring the rifle!"

A small man came through the cabin door. He was holding a semiautomatic rifle by the barrel.

"Set it on the deck, muzzle toward yourself."

The man complied. Kristi didn't think he looked overly concerned about having guns pointed at him. *Maybe he's done this before*, she thought.

"Now, back away." Turning toward her, he said, "Kristi, make sure it's unloaded, then remove the bolt."

The man backed off, then Kristi removed the magazine and opened the bolt. A live round popped out. She quickly accessed the bolt and removed it, rendering the gun useless.

"Your name," Vince said to the captain.

"Stone. Craig Stone. And I greatly resent not only being stopped but the insinuation that I would be carrying any sort of contraband."

"You will have my apologies if it turns out we were misinformed. Have everyone assemble here."

Stone stuck his head inside the cabin and said for everyone to come on deck. He picked up a remote and turned to Vince. "You don't mind if I turn off the entertainment, do you?" as he pushed a button. Somewhere below, a motor whirred. Stone smiled. "There. All quiet now."

The guests filed out onto the deck. The last one out looked familiar to her.

"I demand to know what's going on here," he said.

"We are from the United States Coast Guard on an authorized mission to interdict contraband. This vessel is suspected of carrying such contraband," said Vince.

"I am Lieutenant Commander Steve Bond of the United States Coast Guard. I demand you leave this boat immediately!"

"No, sir. Our orders come from a higher authority. Please join the others," said Vince.

Bond started to approach, but Vince moved the muzzle toward him. Bond quickly retreated and cowered behind one of the women.

A Coast Guard response boat with four men aboard appeared and tied up. The men came aboard. One asked, "Who's in charge?

Vince raised his hand. He motioned to Craig Stone. "This is the captain and owner of the vessel."

The man turned to Stone, "Sir, under the authority of the United States, I am going to search this vessel for contraband."

Steve Bond appeared. "This is ridiculous. These people are my friends."

"Then you know not to interfere in official business." He turned to the other three who boarded with him, "Begin."

The three men began searching everywhere, opening cabinets and chests and tapping on various structure parts.

"What's in there?" asked Vince, pointing to a bench seat covered with a cushion.

"Nothing," said Stone. "It's for bait. We don't have any this trip. So, we're using it for seating."

Vince walked over and pulled off the cushion. There was a lock securing the lid. "Open it."

Stone walked over, and with a smile on his face, took a key and unlocked the lid. Vince flipped it open. Neat bundles wrapped in clear plastic practically filled the space. He looked at Stone, who had a shocked look on his face.

"We've been tricked! Somebody put those there! I don't know how," he began to say.

"Probably," said Vince with a smile, "your bait dump didn't work when you pushed the button on the remote."

Steve Bond appeared. "What!? What!?"

"You've apparently been consorting with drug smugglers, Mr. Bond," said Vince.

Bond's face turned ashen. "No. No. This can't be." He became more agitated. Then, he rushed to the side of the boat, jumped overboard, coughed and sputtered as he took in a mouthful of sea water, and started swimming away.

"Where does he think he's going?" asked Kristi.

"Beats me," said Vince. "California is over there," he said, pointing in a different direction. "Nine miles away. He should make Canada in about two weeks."

"Should we go after him?"

"Probably. It won't hurt to let him wear himself out a little bit. Let me check with the Lieutenant."

Forty

Kristi left the small conference room to get a cup of tea. As she turned the corner, she ran into Lieutenant Commander Christianson.

"Well," said Christianson, "look who we have here. It seems like you forgot who you were working for somewhere along the line. Our deal was that you would tell me what Chief Ayala was doing, and I would write you a good endorsement for the commission program. You didn't hold up your end of the agreement, so you can kiss that endorsement goodbye. In fact, I think your next evaluation may just be bad enough that you never get a chance to go for a commission. Maybe even make it hard for you to stay in the service."

"I was ordered not to say anything to anyone about the mission, and that included you – ma'am. I decided the needs of the service and my country were above what you wanted me to do. Even if it means I won't get your endorsement."

"You'll have to live with that decision. Right now, I have to see if I can help my friend and fellow officer, Steve Bond, get out of the trouble you people created."

"I didn't put him on the boat, ma'am, and he didn't have to jump overboard. That doesn't make him look innocent."

"I'm sure he didn't have anything to do with this smuggling," said Christianson. She turned and entered the inquiry room.

Kristi went to a table set up in an alcove and poured hot water into a cup. She dropped in a tea bag and waited a few minutes. Her stomach was churning. She'd done the right thing, but the right thing may have just ended her career. She pulled the teabag out of the cup, put in a bit of honey and a squeeze of lemon, then returned to the inquiry room. She walked past a sign that read, "Authorized Personnel Only," and entered the room. A sentry posted at the door had checked her in earlier and nodded to her as she entered.

She took a seat next to Vince, leaned toward him, and whispered, "I just saw Commander Christianson. She isn't very happy with me. If she has her way, I'll be working fast food when this enlistment is up."

"Don't worry about her," he whispered back, "you did the right thing."

Captain Yarrow entered the room and took his position behind a table. Four other officers were already seated. Before sitting, he said, "This is an informal inquiry into the events of June 18th. As such, we will waive the rules of evidence and just try to determine the facts. Commander Gardener from the Judge Advocate Generals Office," he said, nodding at an officer at one end of the table, "will ensure we don't run roughshod over anyone's constitutional rights." He nodded to a lieutenant and said, "call the first person."

The lieutenant looked at a paper in his hand and said, "Chief Petty Officer Vincent Ayala."

Vince rose, walked to the front of the room, and took a seat at the small table facing the board. The lieutenant swore him in.

"State your full name and rank for the record."

"Marine Law Enforcement Specialist Chief Petty Officer Vincent Ayala."

"Please tell us in your own words, Chief Ayala, what happened on the afternoon of June 18th," said Captain Yarrow.

Vince related the events as they had occurred.

"And you found the hidden drugs?" he asked.

"I had the captain and owner open a locked bait box built into the boat. We found ten packages, about twenty pounds each, wrapped in clear plastic when Mr. Stone opened it. The contents of the packages were subsequently tested and found to contain both marijuana and cocaine."

"Objection." It was counsel sitting next to Steve Bond at another table. "This witness has no direct knowledge," he started.

"Don't worry. We'll get the chain of custody and chemical analysis sorted out," said Yarrow. "Chief, didn't the bait box have a dumping feature?"

"Uh, yes, sir, it did, but for some reason, it failed. Otherwise, they could have easily dumped the contraband."

"Objection."

Yarrow waved him off with his hand. "Save it for the trial, if there is one." He looked at Vince, "Is there anything else?"

"Yes, sir. Petty Officer First Class Kristi Swanson, also from Sandy Bay, assisted in this action. With her assistance, we were able to stop and board this vessel before the search team led by Lieutenant Baylor arrived. She should be commended for her bravery and action."

"Duly noted, Chief. You are dismissed. Next witness."

"Lieutenant Francis Baylor."

The lieutenant Kristi recognized from the boarding and search party walked to the table, passing Vince on his way back to his seat.

Vince took his seat, and as Lieutenant Baylor was being sworn and stating his name, she whispered to him, "Thank you. You didn't have to do that." There was a warm glow inside her.

"It's the very least I could do," he said, "besides, all I did was tell the truth. You made it possible. And, you did a great job."

Lieutenant Baylor gave his report, including using his response boat to retrieve Lieutenant Commander Steve Bond from the Pacific Ocean after he had jumped from the ship and tried to swim away.

Then, the laboratory technician who had performed the tests on the packages found was called, followed by one of the specialists who testified that the chain of custody had not been broken.

Kristi looked over and saw Steve Bond. His face was taut. He would whisper to his counsel and listen intently as his counsel whispered to him. Two rows back sat Lieutenant Commander Christianson.

"We have one more witness before we take a break," said Yarrow.

A curvy woman wearing a conservative black skirt suit entered the room and took a seat at the table. She had brown hair. A man in a well-tailored suit accompanied her.

"For the record, state your name."

"Susanna Stone."

Kristi looked at Steve Bond. His skin had turned ashen.

"You are here voluntarily?" asked Yarrow.

"Yes."

"Your Honor," started the man accompanying her.

"It's just captain. Captain Yarrow."

The man looked slightly confused. Then, "Mrs. Stone has agreed to testify both here and in civilian court. She did not know," he began.

Captain Yarrow waved him off with one hand. Then to Susanna stone, "Very well. What is your relationship with Mr. Bond?" Yarrow asked.

"I had sex with him to induce him to provide me with information beneficial to my husband's business. At the time, I didn't know my husband's activities were illegal."

The small room erupted. After five minutes, Captain Yarrow ordered the room emptied.

Forty-one

In the hallway, Vince was holding a cup of coffee. Kristi, a cup of tea.

Vince sipped his coffee, then said to her, "I guess there is only one question left concerning Steve Bond."

"What question is that?" she asked.

"Did he do it knowingly, or is he just a dupe. It means the difference between the end of a career or jail time. In this case, it's best to be stupid."

"You don't think he's dumb enough to be involved in drug smuggling," she started.

"It's been known to happen."

"By the way," she said, "I wonder why the dump doors on the bait box didn't work."

"Your guess is as good as mine," he said.

She sipped her tea and gave him side-eyes.

The doors to the inquiry room opened, and the sentry indicated people could reenter.

As they took their seats, Captain Yarrow said to the group, "If everyone can maintain order, we can continue. If not, we'll clear the room. Do I make myself clear?" Then to Susanna Stone, seated with her attorney in the front row, "Mrs. Stone, please retake your place at the table. If you would please, continue with your explanation."

Susanna Stone took her seat. "Well, sir, about once a month, sometimes more often, my husband would take business contacts out on our boat, the Gypsy D, and throw a party. Networking and such, you know. They would play cards – for more money than I like to think about. They drank, smoked cigars, and, I think, the occasional joint. I hate to admit it, but Craig even brought along women for the other men. All to keep his investors happy. You understand. Boys will be boys. I figured it was just business."

Yarrow was silent. Kristi looked around the room and didn't see Lieutenant Commander Christianson.

She leaned to Vince and whispered, "Hey, I don't see the OIC."

"No surprise there," he whispered back, "all of a sudden, her good friend is like a millstone around her neck."

"Well," Susanna continued, "he had done quite well in business. This group of investors has made a substantial profit. Including Steve," she nodded to Steve Bond, who was pale and attempting to make himself smaller in his seat. "I'm sure he didn't have any idea the money was coming from unlawful activities. I didn't even know. I had no idea my husband wasn't engaged in routine investments."

"So," asked Yarrow, "what sort of information did Mr. Bond provide?"

"Well, Craig, my husband, said that if I could find out when and where the Coast Guard patrols were, then he wouldn't have to worry about the authorities crashing his parties. His investors are all important people, some civic leaders. It would have ruined their careers if the news reported they had found to be on a boat gambling and with marijuana and women who weren't their wives."

"And to get this information?"

"Well, sir, we had sex. Three or four times each time, he came over. Once or twice a week for the last month."

Kristi looked at Steve Bond. He was shrinking in the chair.

"And he gave you this information?"

"Yes. He said he tried to get it at headquarters, is that right? He said he got some of the information from a friend of his at one of the outlying stations."

"And your husband knew about this arrangement?"

"Yes, sir, a couple of times he was in the main house while I met Steve in the carriage house."

"Thank you, Mrs. Stone. We appreciate your cooperation." He nodded, and Susanna and her lawyer left the room.

221

"Mr. Bond," said Yarrow. Bond's head snapped up. His lower lip was quivering. "I was going to call you to get your version of the events of June 18th. However, it would seem that with the testimony of Mrs. Stone, there are some actual and additional potential violations of the Uniform Code of Military Justice. I will recommend a full investigation of your activities and that if sufficient evidence is found, a general court-martial be initiated. You should engage legal counsel to ensure adequate defense of these charges. This inquiry is dismissed."

As Yarrow left the room, what had been an undercurrent of murmuring became a cacophony.

"So, what," Kristi started.

"Adultery," said Vince. "Stupid rule we have to live with, but having sex with a married woman who isn't married to you is a violation of the UCMJ, even if he isn't married himself. And they can get him for conduct unbecoming an officer. Jumping overboard when the drugs were found makes him look like a buffoon. Just the so-called recreational marijuana they were smoking might mean jail time. His career is over. If they find evidence he knew they were smuggling drugs, it will be off to Fort Leavenworth for twenty years."

"Jesus."

"Yeah. Christianson may be collateral damage. She will be in hot water if he got operational intel from her and passed it along. Probably not jail time, especially if she can convince the powers that be that she had no idea he was passing it along, but it won't look good on her record. Letter of reprimand at the very least, I would guess."

"This is unbelievable. Is that why she left?"

"Yeah. All of a sudden, her friend was a great liability because of his stupidity."

A lieutenant approached.

"Chief Ayala?"

"Yes, sir."

"Please come with me." The lieutenant turned and started to walk away.

Vince looked at Kristi. "Could you wait for me? For a few minutes? If I'm gone more than ten, go ahead and head home."

"Uh, sure," she said, "do you have any idea what this is for?"

"No. I can't think of anything I've done lately that was terribly wrong," he said with a smile.

She went to the ladies' room and got another cup of tea. Fifteen minutes later, Vince returned.

"So," she started.

"You're not going to believe this," he said. "Starting ten minutes ago, Lieutenant Commander Christianson was pulled back to headquarters where she will be placed into a meaningless administrative position while an investigation is underway."

"What!"

"Yeah. You can dump that tea. I need – we need something stronger."

"Why?"

"Because you're looking at the temporary officer in charge of Sandy Bay Coast Guard Station."

Forty-two

Vince yawned and stretched as he sat at the desk in the OIC's office. He was sifting through piles of documents. He'd been at it for – he checked his watch – three hours. Had it only been three hours? It had seemed like days. He stretched again and picked up his coffee cup. Empty.

There was a knock on the door. He looked up to see Kristi. He waved her in.

She started for the little box on the floor in front of the desk, then paused. There was a small faux Persian rug covering the area.

"Uh, you covered the box?"

"Yeah," he said, "I didn't have time to remove it yet, so I did the next best thing."

"How will the enlisted personnel know where to stand?" she asked, a coy smile on her face.

He motioned to an armchair placed at forty-five degrees.

"In the OIC's office? Are we allowed?" she asked with the same smile.

"Sit," he responded.

"I was going to tell you how positively executive you look," she said, "but if you're going to mingle with the lower classes."

"Don't start," he replied. "If you want to know why I've avoided doing the things I would have needed to get promoted, or God forbid, commissioned, you're looking at it. The only thing missing is a mind-numbing meeting with a group of people I don't like who are all fighting for the next promotion."

"Yes, and it makes you grouchy."

He gave her a faux stern look and raised one eyebrow.

She looked up to see Agent Collins enter the bay. Collins was wearing a black pantsuit, white blouse, and sunglasses, which she removed. Her hair was in a ponytail. Kristi thought it made her look about fifteen years old, but then there was the gun and the badge. And her eyes. Collins' eyes had an older look, like someone who had seen a lot of bad things. She looked around, spotted Kristi and Vince, and headed toward them.

Collins entered the office and sat in an empty chair. "How are you liking your new gig?" she asked Vince.

"I hate it. Three hours here is an eternity. I'd much rather be getting wet and dirty."

"I know the feeling," she said with a smile.

"Would you like something to drink?" asked Vince.

"Please. Tea? Hot?"

"I'll get it," offered Kristi.

"Actually," said Collins, "I'd like to have a couple of minutes with Petty Officer Swanson if I might."

"No problem," said Vince. "I'll pop over to the lounge. Just give me the high sign when you want me back." He got up and left the office.

"I wanted to get your thoughts on a couple of things. So, you remember boarding the Gypsy D?"

"I'll never forget it," answered Kristi.

"Run me through it if you would."

"Well, we were approaching the boat. I was at the helm of the Bayliner. Vince, that is, Chief Ayala, hailed them with the bull horn. They fired a few rounds at us."

"How'd that make you feel?" asked Collins.

"How'd it make me feel? I was scared as hell. I've never been shot at before."

"And what did you do?"

Kristi thought a few seconds. "I think I crouched down a little. I thought about getting out of there, but we were on a mission. I looked at Vince, the chief, for direction. He told me to increase our speed and pull closer to the Gypsy D. So I did. He pulled out a rifle, fired a few rounds across their bow, and ordered them to heave-to. They did."

"How were you doing?"

"My heart was pounding. I don't think I was as scared right then. We were busy. We had things to do."

"And you decided to board at that time?"

"Well, Vince," she said, then started to change it to the chief, but Collins stopped her, saying, "Vince is fine."

Kristi smiled, then said, "Vince is encouraging me to get a commission, so he asked me my opinion about boarding right away or waiting for LT Baylor. He said if we waited, they would have more time to dump any contraband. Going aboard immediately would be potentially more hazardous. He said I'd be making these decisions in the future, so I might as well get used to making them. I chose to board immediately, and we did."

"How did the captain, uh owner, of the vessel seem when you boarded?" asked Collins.

"He was all self-righteous, claiming he'd done nothing wrong. Then that officer, Bond, came out and ordered us off the boat."

"So, after you found the drugs, what did the captain do?" asked Collins.

"First, he claimed they must have been planted, but in about ten seconds, he clammed up. He said he needed to make a call. When he was told he couldn't, he became almost catatonic. Why?" asked Kristi.

"I've got a couple of things I thought were interesting. First, after he was booked, his wife showed up. When he learned she was here to see him, the first words out of his mouth were, 'What does she want?' Not exactly what you'd expect."

"Yeah. You'd think he'd be happy to see a friendly face."

"Exactly," said Collins. She pulled her phone out of her pocket. "Then, there's this." She clicked a button and turned the screen toward Kristi.

There was a split-screen. It showed Craig Stone on one side of a glass barrier and Susanna Stone on the other. They were talking through a telephone system.

Craig slowly picked up the handset. "I'm sorry. I didn't," he started, but Susanna cut him off.

"Don't say a word. Everything you say is recorded. You understand?" she said. Her tone was authoritative.

He nodded and dropped his head.

"We'll get you an attorney. Until then, don't say anything. Anything. Understand? Don't say anything that the attorney doesn't want you to say. They'll tell you they can help you if you talk, but it isn't true. Try to stay strong. Act like a man for once. I'll be in touch." She hung up the phone and left the booth.

The guard came for Stone.

"So," said Collins, "thoughts?"

"From what I saw on the Gypsy D, I'd say his wife runs pretty much everything in their house," answered Kristi. "And there were no questions about how he was doing or apparent feelings of sympathy."

"And outside the house? What do you think are the chances he'd run a drug smuggling operation without his wife knowing about it?"

"Pretty small. I'd think she would have at least known about it." Kristi paused. "So, do you think she's involved, and her only reason to visit him is to make sure he keeps silent? That would seem to make sense."

"One other thing. When one of our male agents questioned him, he seemed fairly composed. When Agent Way and I questioned him, he was completely withdrawn, almost fearful."

"So," said Kristi, "he's afraid of women. I wonder why." She turned to Collins, "Okay, but why did you come to me? You must have seen the same things I did and come to the same conclusions."

"I did. You seem bright. The Bureau is always looking for sharp women. You're clean. And smart. You'd need a degree, but there are ways we could help you out. When you get within a year of your obligation, give me a call," said Collins, handing her a card. "We'll see if we can convince you to join our ranks. I'll be in touch." Collins shook her hand.

They waved to Vince, then Collins turned to her and asked, "Is he seeing anyone?"

Kristi's hackles went up, but she couldn't admit she and Vince had been together. She couldn't say she was in love with him. "Uh no, I don't know."

"Could be a lot of fun for a while. Maybe longer than a while. You know? It'd be nice to have that under the covers to keep you warm on a cold winter night."

Vince returned with a tray and three cups. Hot tea for Collins and coffee for himself and Kristi.

"So, we've been interviewing Lieutenant Commander Bond. He's lawyered up, but we've gotten some information out of him. He says they had sex, usually in the carriage house. We asked about the sex, but he wasn't forthcoming. I guess he didn't want to provide a blow by blow," she said deadpan.

"He did mention one odd thing," she continued. "A couple of times, she had to throw a robe on and take care of something at the main building. Like meeting the grocery delivery boy."

"So, they were having sex, and she needed to greet the grocery boy?" asked Kristi.

"Yeah. Weird, right? So, we interviewed him. He's thrilled to deliver her groceries. Twice a week. She tips very well, and when pressed, he admitted that once a month or so, he gets a happy ending."

"What the hell?" asked Vince.

"Yeah. He's even passed up a promotion. Who wouldn't? He figures his benefits are better as a delivery boy. We're keeping him under surveillance, but I think he's clean. We're also keeping her under surveillance. We don't think she's as innocent as she pretends, but we hope she'll lead us to the next level. That's about all for now. I'll try to keep you in the loop.

She finished her tea and got up. "Chief, can I talk to you for a moment?"

Vince got up and followed her out of the office.

Kristi watched as Collins turned to face him. She was smiling, leaning forward. Kristi's heart was pounding as her body tensed. It took all her will to stay seated. Yes, she was mad. Collins had invaded her territory, and Kristi wanted her gone.

Collins pulled something from her pocket. A card? She took a pen, wrote something on it, and then handed it to Vince. She smiled and touched his arm, then turned and walked away.

After she was gone, Vince looked at the card, then put it into his pocket.

Kristi's heart sank. Her throat was thick, and tears were forming in her eyes.

Vince returned to the office and plopped into the desk chair.

Kristi started to speak, but had to clear her throat, then asked, "What did she want, if it isn't confidential?"

"She talked about getting together for a drink sometime." His voice was nonchalant. "How about you. What did she talk to you about?"

She showed him the card. "Said she wanted my thoughts. Ended up making a pitch for the Bureau." She wiped the tears from her eyes.

"You'd probably do well. Thinking about it?" he asked. Then, "Are you okay?"

"Yeah, just something in my eye." Then, "I don't know. Agent Collins doesn't seem to be a very happy person. Besides, I've got a couple of years before I could even consider it. Still," she said, "there is the badge and the gun."

"Don't forget the handcuffs," said Vince, smiling.

"Oh, I've got those," she said. "Pink and fuzzy. I'd still like to show them to you sometime." She felt a little lighter talking and joking. Just the two of them, but she deflated. The question nagged at her. Why did he have to put the card into his pocket?

Forty-three

Kristi walked to Annie's office and knocked on the open door.

"Hi! Come on in," Annie said.

Kristi walked to one of the chairs, plopped down, and then slumped.

"Well, you don't look very chipper," said Annie. "What's up?"

"When Agent Collins talked to me, Vince got us coffee and tea. She asked if he was seeing anyone. I figure she's FBI and has ways of telling if people are lying. I panicked. I couldn't say, 'Yeah, me, bitch, hands off.' So, I said I didn't know. She started making comments about how much fun it would be and how nice it would be to have him as a bed warmer. I started to get these pictures, then I got mad, but I couldn't say anything. I'd be hanging us both. I don't know if she saw me turning red."

"Well, of course, you got mad. You care for him, even if you can't tell anyone. He cares for you too. And, of course, the pictures you have are of the two of you. You don't want her in any of those pictures."

"But, after we all finished talking, she said she wanted to see him for a minute. They went out into the bay, and I could tell she was putting on the full-court press. Smiling, flipping her hair, leaning toward him. Hands on her hips, elbows back so her boobs would push out. I could feel myself getting madder and madder. Then, she pulled out one of her cards, wrote something on the back, and handed it to him."

"What did he do?"

"He put it into his pocket. He kept it."

"Well," said Annie, "you couldn't expect him to rip it into shreds and throw it into her face."

"It would have made me feel better. When he came back into the office, I asked him what she wanted. He said she wanted to go out for drinks. He should have thrown the card away right then, but he didn't." Tears were filling her eyes. "I mean, I know right now, the whole superior-subordinate relationship makes it so we can't be together. But I thought maybe we could find a way. When I'm around him, when we talk, it feels great. To think some woman will come swooping in and," she began to cry.

Annie pulled a tissue from a box and handed it to Kristi, and then went to the cabinet with the one-cupper. She returned and handed Kristi a cup. "There. Drink that. You'll feel better."

Kristi took a healthy sip and then started to cough. "What the hell?"

"Whiskey. Medicinal. What did you think? That I was going to get you tea? When the chips are down, chamomile is not my style."

"I'm going to have to hide out for the rest of the day now," said Kristi.

"Might as well finish it then," said Annie. "You can hide out here, or we can leave and do something else. It'll give us time to brainstorm." She paused, then, "One thing we could do is let Collins know he is seeing someone, and if she asks who, we can say it's me. We'd have to sell it, though. She might be watching. So – just for you," Annie said, smiling at her, "I'd be willing to spend a few nights with him, you know, to convince her. I'd have to look completely worn out coming out of his place."

Kristi just stared.

"Not buying it, huh? I thought it was worth a try, but see, you're already feeling a little better."

"Actually, I'm feeling kind of helpless."

"Hey," said Annie, "now you've got me to help out. We'll find a way. After all, I was able to wangle the orders to the San Lorenzo so you two could be together. Don't underestimate me."

"Yeah," said Kristi. "You never told me just how you managed to do that."

"I've got my secrets and connections."

Forty-four

Vince studied the piles of documents in front of him. He'd taken a couple of breaks, but what he wanted to do was get into a boat and head out to sea. At the very least, do some maintenance on a boat or the pier. He stretched again and picked up his coffee cup. Empty. He needed more coffee. He decided the walk to the farthest coffee maker in the bay when Kristi appeared.

"You're not getting very far with this," she said, smiling.

"Every time I finish something, Annie has something else. Man, I hate this."

"The XO would say that this is an important part of running the service."

"Then, he should get someone who wants to do it."

She shrugged. "I'm not sure anyone wants to do it."

Another knock on the door. Annie entered without waiting for approval. She had a mug in her hand.

"Thought you could use a little pick-me-up," she said with a smile, setting the mug on the desk and turning the handle toward him.

"Do I ever." He picked up the mug and took a healthy swig, then coughed. "Old family recipe?"

"Um, yes. I hope you like it."

"What recipe?" asked Kristi.

"Unless I miss my guess, it calls for a healthy portion of Jameson's," he said.

Annie shrugged.

"I've had that recipe," said Kristi.

"You know, I'm not supposed to be drinking on duty," he said.

"Yes," replied Annie, laughing. "And anyone doing so will find him or herself in the OIC's office."

He shook his head.

"So," she said, "any of that stuff making sense?"

"Yeah, it's just mind-numbing looking through it all. How'd Christianson do it?"

"She had me do most of it. She had no interest," replied Annie.

Kristi was laughing.

"Then why," he started.

"Because she didn't care. You need to be familiar with this stuff. I'll take care of the grunt work. Let me know what you need to have done."

"I don't think we pay you enough, Annie."

"I know you don't. By the way, did you get to the blue folder?" Annie asked.

"Uh, no," he said, looking through the pile.

"There."

Vince picked up the file and opened it. He read for a moment, then said, "No!"

"Come as a surprise?" asked Annie.

"What?" asked Kristi.

"I don't believe this," he said. "The Coast Guard has always been the red-headed stepchild when it came to the budget, but our next year will be leaner, if you can believe that – than last year's. As a money-saving strategy, they're thinking of closing some of the smaller stations. Ours is one of them."

"You're kidding. Right?" said Kristi. "I mean, they can't close this station."

"They can and will," he said. "Did Christianson respond to this?" he asked, looking at Annie. "She's supposed to submit a report with all the things – reasons – that Sandy Bay is essential to the mission."

"No. She wants to get back to a large facility where she can get in line for a promotion. She considers this a backwater assignment. She doesn't care about Sandy Bay. Maybe she thinks she'll get back to Valhalla sooner if they close this place.

Right now, she's kind of fighting for her career, and I'm sure she doesn't care about Sandy Bay closing."

"So, if they close Sandy Bay," started Kristi.

"They can't take care of the mission from headquarters," said Vince, "and we all get shipped out to far-flung places."

"And, I may be out of a job entirely," said Annie. "I don't want to go to headquarters and sit in the typing pool. The other ladies may see me as a threat."

"Typing pool?" asked Kristi.

"Figure of speech," said Annie.

"Isn't there anything we can do?" asked Kristi.

"I'll have to give it some thought," said Vince. "We can start by getting a list of all the rescues this station has made in the last year." He took another swig of his coffee. "Thanks for this."

"I figured you could use it. I would have brought two if I knew you had company. Anyway, I'll let you get back to it." She stood and left the room, closing the door behind her.

"That's just," said Kristi, not sure how to finish the sentence.

"Yeah," he said. "I – I kinda look forward to seeing you. I know we'll all go in different directions someday. I just didn't want it to be soon."

"Me too," she said quietly. There was water in her eyes.

They sat quietly for a few minutes. Then, he started looking through the papers again. He stopped and studied one.

"Well, this is interesting," said Vince.

"What?"

"That boat. The one that you rescued the family from."

"Yeah. The Francine. When I talked to Commander Cruise on the San Lorenzo, she said they might have found it. While they were doing some mapping of the sea floor."

"Turns out it's in about two hundred feet of water. On a seamount." He paused. "It might be interesting to look at just what the damage was."

"So, how are you going to do that? An RUV?"

"Be nice if we had one. No. Two hundred is a little deep for air, but I think I'd like to dive her. Take a look. Get some pictures."

"I've got my certificate. I could go along and,"

"No way. You've got a new certificate for about seventy feet. Max. Along the shore. Maybe out of a dive boat. With a guide. This is different. It's open ocean. There's nothing until you hit bottom. If you get turned around, you may be heading for Japan, Canada, Mexico, or the thousand-foot bottom."

"But you can't do it alone." Her voice was insistent.

"Sure. I'll have somebody on the boat."

"You mean somebody in addition to me."

"Yes, ma'am. McPherson," he said, nodding his head toward her.

"What if something goes wrong. I'd hate to think,"

"You'd hate to think that if anything happened to me, you might be the one looking at all this," he said, running his hand over the pile on the desk.

"You know that isn't what I meant."

"Yes. Don't worry. Nothing will go wrong."

Forty-five

Vince awakened in a cold sweat. He'd had a dream. More appropriately, a nightmare. He'd been diving on a sunken boat, deep in the ocean. The light was dim, and he was entangled in a fishing net. He reached for his knife to cut his way out, but the sheath was empty. His air was almost gone, and he panicked.

He knew why he'd had the dream. The upcoming deep solo dive he was going to do today and a memory from years ago. As part of a volunteer diving team, he'd recovered the body of a man who died while diving solo on a wreck. That man hadn't taken precautions and had been trapped in a fishing net he was foolish enough to swim under. He'd gotten tangled and had no help to free himself. His dive knife lay on the ocean floor a few feet from him. Vince never forgot the look on his face.

He pulled himself out of bed and headed for the shower. Afterward, he dressed and headed for his car. He drove to Kristi's apartment and parked. He crossed the lot and climbed the stairs to the second floor. Kristi opened the door before his third knock.

"Good morning," he said.

"Good morning." She walked into the living area and turned back toward him. Her left arm was across her body, grasping her right elbow. She looked at him, then at the floor. "I don't want you to do this," she said quietly.

"You don't have to go," he answered.

"That's – that's not the point," she said. "It would be even harder being here. Not knowing if," she said, stepping close to him. Her eyes searched his face.

"I'm taking precautions – every precaution I can. I'll be fine."

"If anything happens," she said, moving against him and wrapping her arms around him. Her head was against his chest. She looked up at him. "I could go along. On the dive."

"We talked about this. I can do it fine, but it isn't a dive for a novice sport diver."

She released him and walked away. She picked up a sweatshirt and put it on. They walked to the door in silence. She looked at him furtively. She left first, and he started to close the door.

"Remember the security code?" she asked.

"Yeah," he said, keying it in.

They drove in silence to the station and parked in the senior NCO's spot.

"Don't you want to park in the OIC's spot?" she asked.

"I'm hoping that assignment won't be for very long, and I don't want to get used to parking there."

He pulled a dive bag out of the trunk and headed for the pier. McPherson was there, loading gear onto a small response boat. Kristi counted six SCUBA tanks, two sets of two and two singles, all with regulators attached.

"Why so many?" she asked.

"I'll need a set of doubles for the dive itself. A dive like this requires a couple of stops on the way up. I'll stop at thirty feet for five minutes and twenty feet for twenty minutes. When I come back up, I'll be running short of air, so we'll have a fresh tank tied at thirty feet."

"And those?" she asked, pointing at the second set of doubles.

"I'll be using those," said McPherson, "but only if I have to."

"What does he mean, 'only if I have to,' Vince?" she demanded, looking at him.

"Okay." It was McPherson. "He's got fifteen minutes bottom time, and the bottom time starts when he leaves the surface. So, in reality, he's got about ten on the bottom. When he gets there, he'll send up a pink balloon. When he leaves the bottom, he'll send up a white one. He'll stop for two minutes at one hundred feet, then rise to his first decompression stop at thirty, where he'll get a fresh tank and send up a yellow balloon. That way, we'll know where he is and check his progress with the dive plan."

245

"You haven't explained the second set of doubles," she said.

"He's also got a red balloon. That one means things aren't going according to plan. If he pops the red one, I don those and head down."

"What!"

"It's just a precaution," said Vince. "I'm going to be careful down there. I've worked out the stops so I can double-check my dive computer. Maybe I shouldn't have told you."

"Don't even think that way," she said quickly.

"Let's go," Vince said to McPherson.

McPherson started the engines, and Vince threw off the lines. They headed out of the bay into the ocean.

The water was calm, and they reached the GPS coordinates within forty-five minutes. McPherson used sonar to check they were in the right spot. "We were lucky," he said. "The top of this thing is only half the size of a football field. I'm amazed the boat landed here."

McPherson dropped the anchor. He dropped a shot line marked at twenty and thirty feet. He grabbed two of the single tanks and put one on. He put on a mask and said, "Be right back," before falling over the side. He was back in less than five minutes. "Spare's in place."

Vince was already in his wet suit. He had a dive knife strapped to the inside of one calf and a smaller one on his chest.

He slid on his fins, and McPherson helped him with the tanks. Vince picked up two underwater lights.

"No weight belt?" asked Kristi.

"Lead shot held in the tank connector. I pull the release, the shot goes out, and I come up. One less belt to worry about."

McPherson checked that the air was on. Vince checked the pressure.

Vince had a small camera. He took a look around, gave a smile, and said, "See you in about forty minutes." He put the regulator into his mouth, took a breath to make sure it worked, gave the diver's okay sign, and stepped back.

Before she could respond, he fell backward over the side and swam underwater toward the shot line. "Don't go, please," she whispered.

Forty-six

Cold water filled Vince's wet suit. As always, he shivered at first. Then, his body warmed the water trapped by the suit. It kept him warm and created buoyancy, but the increasing water pressure would compress the rubber to practically nothing as he descended to two hundred feet. That meant no added buoyancy and almost no thermal insulation. He could compensate for the buoyancy, but he'd be cold. It was another reason not to overstay.

He passed the twenty-foot mark and headed for thirty. The decompression stop tank was in place, clipped to the shot line. He cleared his ears and breathed into his mask to equalize the pressure. He passed the tank and headed for the bottom as quickly as possible. His bottom time started at the surface, and the faster he could get to the bottom, the more time he'd have there.

The shot line disappeared into a dark gray-blue nothing. As he descended, the light became dimmer, and he was surrounded by that same dark gray-blue. He'd often wondered what was lurking out there, just beyond his vision, unknown to him. He knew he wasn't unknown to whatever it was. The clattering of his exhaust bubbles told every creature in the ocean just where he was.

Slowly, something dark was coming into view. The seamount. Like everything else, it was dark. Dark brown. Mud probably. He'd have to be careful not to stir it up with his movements. If he did, visibility would turn to nothing, and the dive would be over.

Visibility was decent, if not great, although it was dark, like the time after the sun went down just before total darkness. He paused twenty feet above the bottom. There was a slow current. The silt cloud from the anchor hitting bottom had dissipated. He put a small puff of air into the balloon marked "pink" and let it go. He knew beforehand he wouldn't be able to tell pink from white down here. He looked around. The target wasn't in the immediate vicinity, and he didn't have any time to waste. He looked around and thought he saw something light on the edge of his vision. He clipped a safety cord to the shot line. It would help him find his way back. At the same time, it would keep him from drifting away in the current.

He swam in the direction he hoped would bring him to the Francine. After about ten feet, the former pleasure craft appeared out of the gloom. It was sitting upright with the bow perched on a rock. The boat was at about a twenty-degree angle. He'd lucked out. Almost the entire hull was exposed.

He swam to it carefully, ten feet off the bottom. He swam slowly around it, clicking off photo after photo as he went. Then, he took a chance and descended lower, circling again for more photos. He took these closer to the wreck. He let himself sink just above the bottom and pulled out his dive knife, using it to pull himself along rather than stirring up mud with his fins.

He inspected the hull as quickly as he could. There was no damage he could see. He looked at his watch. Less than five minutes remained. He used his buoyancy compensator to lift him off the bottom, then moved to the cockpit and cabin. A few fish bolted from the cabin as he peered in and took some shots. He moved to the cockpit and opened the engine hatch. He looked inside quickly, then took four quick shots. He checked his watch as he swam to the cabin. Less than a minute of his bottom time remained. Going into the cabin was dangerous, but he wanted to check one more thing.

He flashed his light around and found the head. He pulled open the door and stuck his body in. It was old-fashioned. Inflow line and valve. Outflow. He reached over. The outflow was secure. Then the inflow. It was open. He took two more photos, then backed out of the space and swam to the cabin opening. He was far from the shot line but started to ascend as he pulled himself toward it along the safety cord. He checked his time. Three minutes over. He hoped he'd still be okay with his calculated decompression times. He'd given himself more time than required. Finally reaching the shot line thirty feet above the bottom, he released the balloon he'd marked "white."

He stopped for two minutes at one hundred feet, a so-called deep stop. He reached the thirty-foot stop and the fresh tank three minutes after leaving the bottom and released the yellow balloon. After five minutes, he ascended to twenty feet. He stayed twenty-five minutes. He checked his dive computer. It agreed that he was safe to surface. He swam slowly to the surface. The sun was warm and bright.

He swam to the boat and removed his tank. McPherson pulled it out of the water. Kristi's hand was there to help him to the ladder. He pulled off his fins and mask and handed them up. He climbed into the boat and plopped down onto the bench, taking a deep breath and unzipping his wet suit top.

"You scared the hell out of us," she said. "That damn white balloon was three minutes overdue. Two more minutes and McPherson would have been in the water heading down. Weren't you paying attention? What were you thinking?"

"I was fine," said McPherson. "I wasn't worried."

"Was that why you were putting on the tanks when the white balloon finally popped up?"

McPherson shrugged.

Vince looked at her and smiled. "There were a couple more things I had to check. At the last minute, something I had to know."

"Well, I hope it was worth it," she said.

"Yeah, well. The boat's sitting upright, with the hull exposed. I didn't see any damage, but we'll double-check the photos. I went over because I needed to check the marine toilet. Somebody left the inflow open. Either somebody made a very stupid mistake," he said.

"Or?" she asked.

"Or they sank the boat intentionally in a storm. They could have all drowned. Begs the question, why?"

Forty-seven

They again sat across the table from Bob Johnson in a small glass-enclosed meeting room in the bank.

"So, what can I do for the Coast Guard today?" he asked.

"We just need to go over a few more things for our report," said Vince.

"I thought that was all taken care of," he said, shifting in his chair. "How much more can there be?"

"Well, because you reported this as an accident, the insurance company wants a detailed report." Vince looked through pages in a folder. "You're sure you hit something in the water."

"Yes. I felt it. I'm sure it cracked the hull. I only wish we could prove that. But no way to do that. The boat is probably sitting in a thousand feet of water," he stopped.

"Well, sir, I have good news and bad news," said Vince.

"Wha – what?"

"Yes," said Kristi. "Even though you were ten miles out, your boat landed on the top of a small seamount. It sits in about two hundred feet of water."

Bob Johnson only stared.

"Chief Ayala was able to dive her. Not an easy dive, but he did."

"And, Mr. Johnson, we were able to take photographs of the Francine," said Ayala, opening a manilla folder and spreading a dozen eight by ten photos across the table. "There is no crack in the hull, but there is an open marine toilet inflow valve."

As Johnson looked at the photographs, his mouth dropped open. Then a tear rolled from his eye and down his cheek. He touched one of the photographs.

"Now," said Vince, "would you like to tell us what really happened?"

Johnson got up from the table, walked to the window overlooking the lobby, and ran his fingers through the hair on both sides of his head. He stood motionless for two minutes. Then, he took a deep breath and returned to the table.

"Okay. What do you want to know?"

"What did you do, and why?" asked Vince.

"I've got a problem."

"Gambling," said Kristi.

He shot her a quick look, then said, "Yeah. You must have gotten that from my wife. Anyway, I was in way over my head, but I couldn't quit. Then, I get a call. Here, at work. I knew the caller. It was my bookie. He said someone would be in touch.

Someone who'd bought my debt and didn't mess around." He paused. "Man, I could use a drink."

"Anyway," he continued, "When I got the call, it came to my personal line, not through the receptionist. They used something to modify their voice. They said they'd cancel my debt if I did them a little favor. I asked about the favor. They said it wouldn't be anything illegal, but it would help out a friend. I'd know when the time came. The whole thing was scary."

"And," asked Kristi.

"So, a few days later, I got a second call. The same modified voice called my private line. They said I was to take my boat out. They gave me the course. Two eighty degrees. They said they wanted me to take my wife and daughter with me. I asked why. They said she should change out of her pretty blue dress before the trip. I was scared as hell. They knew what my daughter was wearing to school that day. They'd watched my daughter. Probably my wife, too."

Johnson was agitated.

"After an hour, I was to start flooding the boat, call the Coast Guard. So, I opened the inflow and let water in. I let more in than I bargained for. After the engine stopped, I tried to go back in and shut the valve. Stay afloat. But the water was too deep. I couldn't see and couldn't get to it."

He looked at the photographs. "I loved that boat. It wasn't much, but I loved it." He dropped the photo. "Anyway, your little angel saved us. I can't thank you enough," he said, looking at Kristi. "But apparently, they were good to their word. They canceled my debt, and I've been scared straight. No more gambling for me. I gave my wife access to my phone and computer. And, I apologized profusely for my stupidity that night and with the gambling."

Kristi and Vince thanked him and left the bank.

"It makes absolutely no sense," said Vince. "Why send somebody out like that?"

"And why the wife and child?" she asked. "So, what do we do with this information?"

"We'll write up a report and take it to the XO. Maybe he can figure out what's going on."

Vince's phone began to ring. "Chief Ayala – First National Bank – interviewing Bob Johnson – about the sinking of the Francine – Now? – Sure – Fifteen minutes." He punched off. "That was Agent Collins. It seems Mr. Stone had a change of heart. They showed him surveillance of his wife starting to clear out, and he decided to make a statement. They're pulling her in now, and they've invited us to watch through the mirror. Interested?"

"Am I!"

Forty-eight

Kristi and Vince looked through a two-way mirror into the room where Kristi had been questioned earlier. Agents Way and Collins sat on one side of the table. Susanna Stone sat on the other.

Kristi looked at her watch. "They've been at it for forty-five minutes."

"They're wearing her down," he said. "She's getting tired. She might make a mistake and give up what they want."

"So, we offered your husband a deal," said Collins, pushing a folder across the table. "Less time for information. He tells us you were more than an innocent victim. When your husband found out that you were going to leave him holding the bag, he decided to talk."

"So," said Way, "let's go through this again. Your story is that you finally figured out your husband was in big trouble, you might lose everything, and you decided to escape. You got into your car and started out but didn't get very far. Where did you think you were going?"

"And, how were you going to support yourself?" added Collins.

"The bank accounts, the house, the boat, everything has a hold," said Way.

"Fine!" Susanna fairly shouted. "It's all going to come out anyway. It was my business. MY business."

"Your business?" asked Collins as she sat back in her chair and folded her arms against her chest.

"Yeah, my business. Mine. I won't say," she said.

"So, you're saying it wasn't your husband's?" asked Way.

"My husbands?" Susanna said, snorting. "My husband is worthless. He's a façade. A shill. He wouldn't know the first thing about running a business."

"But isn't he the successful investor?"

"Are you kidding? The only reason I needed him was as a front. Easier to think that a man would be able to run a successful investment scheme. Not to mention a drug-smuggling operation. I did both. The money came from the drug business. I made all the arrangements, but I needed a front. To look the part, and, face it, if things went south with the suppliers, it didn't hurt to have them going after him, not me. So, he made the arrangements. He did exactly what I told him to do. Sometimes I actually had to write out the instructions. And, I had to run an investment business to hide the profits from this one."

"So, your investors?" asked Collins. "Did they know where the money was coming from? Really coming from?"

"Most didn't care. Even if they were to give a second thought, they were making money, more than they ever thought possible. Invest a little, get back a lot. Some of the so-called investors were important people. It lent an air of respectability to the thing. They didn't realize they were buying drugs and bribing officials."

"And the parties on the yacht?" asked Way.

"It kept the investors happy and helped create the façade of a successful investment firm. Trips to Mexico where Craig picked up the drugs."

"And you did everything?"

"Mostly. Craig, of course, played the perfect fool. Smiling. Shaking hands. He was like a fraternity rush chair. About as useful, too. But people bought it. You believe what you expect to be true."

"And, you were able to get patrol information out of a Coast Guard officer," Collins sifted through some papers, "Lieutenant Commander Bond?"

"Yeah. Bond," she said, leaning back in her chair. "Another worthless male. Men think they run the world. Women have been running things for millennia. Mostly letting men think they are the ones who are in charge. Show a little boob, flash a little leg, or hint that there might be sex in their future, and most men stop thinking altogether. Pair that with a suggestion or two, and bingo. I gave him a taste of what he must have thought was heaven when we were in the wine cellar during one of our parties. Nothing like a little danger or kink to add to the rush."

"And that's what you did with your husband as well, to get him to agree to your scheme?" asked Way.

"My husband? Maybe a bit at first. Then, I learned that he wanted, needed, a woman in charge. So, I took charge. Really took charge. Of everything. It didn't take long for him to submit. So submissive. Unless we were in public when he got to pretend to be the big man in charge. Otherwise, I kept him on a tight leash. Sometimes literally. I didn't have sex with him," she smirked. "So weak."

"But you did have sex with Mr. Bond when your husband was out of town, on his boat? And this led to information that would aid your smuggling business."

"I got information. He was eager to give it to me. He would have given me the keys to Fort Knox. To get more," she let the thought die. "His information was marginally useful. He got some from one of the bases. He thought the information kept the parties from being busted and his investments growing. He didn't know about the drugs. The information he got from his friend, Christianson, I think her name was, was more useful. She helped us to avoid some of the patrols. We had to resort to other means when necessary. But my husband wasn't always out of town or on his boat. There were times when Bond and I would have sex when Craig was home."

"And he knew?" asked Collins, her eyes opening wide.

"Yes, he knew. I have cameras set up in the carriage house. Direct feed to the main house. I had Craig watch the whole thing on a big screen. I used it to humiliate him. Keep him in line. And, of course, I recorded it, just in case I needed leverage for later. With Bond, I didn't need any more leverage."

"Um, didn't your husband ever leave, I mean the marriage?" asked Way.

"Oh yes. Once. A few years ago. He tried. We convinced him that he should never try that again and let him know there would be consequences if he did. He's been a good boy ever since," she said, smiling.

"We?"

"A friend and me. It was fun." She was smiling.

"You say you used other means, as well, to throw the authorities off?"

"Sure. Like distress calls. A couple of times, we used drones to send out the calls. It made the Coast Guard pull all the resources to save a vessel in distress. If they got close before we could get the drone out of there, we'd just crash it into the ocean. Once or twice, we had to induce someone to take a boat out and issue a call."

Kristi and Vince looked at each other with wide eyes. "Now it starts to make sense. The night the Francine was going down."

"Like the Francine? That family could have died. I don't suppose that bothers you," said Way.

Susanna just shrugged.

After a short pause, "Okay. The day we caught your husband with the contraband," started Way.

"That moron," interrupted Susanna. "He's supposed to check that the bait box is working properly before the pickup on each run. I'm sure he figured he'd never had to use it, and he'd checked it a week or month ago. Then, this trip, when he needed it, it had gotten wedged closed."

Kristi turned her head and looked at Vince. "I don't suppose you know anything about that. Your little swim at the marina?"

He put on an innocent face and shrugged his shoulders. "You followed me?"

"Um, yeah. I guess I did."

After a few minutes, the interview ended, and a guard took Susanna out of the room.

"And they say marriage is dead," said Kristi soberly.

"Yeah. She was sure a manipulator."

"I wonder what they threatened her husband with."

"I don't think I want to know," said Vince.

Forty-nine

As Agents Collins and Way left the interrogation room, they left the observation booth.

"So," said Collins, "you heard."

"Yeah," said Kristi, "she ran the whole thing while pretending to be Little Miss Perfect Housewife, except for where she was having sex with someone other than her husband. Apparently, lots of someones. She's scary."

"Not the worst we've seen," added Way. She paused. "I, that is, we appreciate the help you've given us. It would have taken longer without you."

"But I sense a but coming on," said Vince.

"Now, we'll wrap up a few things, and your part is pretty much finished. You can head back to Sandy Bay. Since it was all done covertly, you shouldn't talk about more than the interdiction at sea, although you might not want to talk about that much either. Retributions happen. Anyway, thank you. We'll let you know if we need you."

"So, what are you going to do now? Prosecute Susanna and Craig? I'm sure there have to be more people involved," said Vince.

"Yeah," said Collins, "We'll go over the surveillance tapes to see what we can find. We think she might have made contact with others in the organization. Nothing came out of the taps on her phones, although she could have a phone that we don't have a record of. So far, there's nothing on any of the computers, either. We might get lucky with the tapes. It'll probably take some time."

"So, thanks, again," said Way.

Vince looked at Kristi and shrugged. "Looks like we're headed back to the base and our work-a-day lives."

As they turned to leave, Agent Collins said, "Uh, chief, could I see you for a minute? You might be able to help with something. I think what I've got will interest you."

Kristi's face turned red, and her eyes narrowed. She didn't like the wording Collins used.

Vince looked at her and said, "I'll catch up with you. Go ahead."

Agent Collins turned to him and said, "Would you mind going over some surveillance films with me? You might see something that I'd miss."

"Uh, sure. No problem, Agent Collins," he said.

She turned, and he followed her down a hallway. "You've been a great asset in this investigation," Kristi heard her say. "And call me Katy. I'd like to convince you to move to our San Diego office." Kristi couldn't hear any response as the door closed behind them.

Fifty

Collins opened the door to a small air-conditioned room with a table in the center. There was a laptop on the table and four large monitors on a facing wall.

"Here, have a seat," she said, taking one of two folding chairs set close together on one side of the table.

Vince pulled out the second chair and seated himself.

Agent Collins powered up the computer, and the four screens on the wall came to life. "Okay," she said, "just try to see if anything strikes you."

"Four screens at once, Agent Collins?" he asked.

"Uh, yes. If anything looks interesting, we'll look at it more closely. Saves time. And it's Katy. Agent Collins seems so formal," she said, sounding casual while looking at the computer keyboard.

Vince sat back and began scanning the images on the four screens. "I'm not sure I'm seeing anything," he said.

"Well, a lot of the videos are filled with nothing interesting. Don't worry about when the target is driving somewhere. It's what she may do when she gets there."

They watched the screens for an hour. Vince's brain was about to shut down. He turned to tell Agent Collins he needed to stop, when something caught his eye.

"Wait a second," he said.

"What?"

"Run that one back," he said, pointing to the upper left screen.

"Uh, wait a second." She played with the keys. After a minute, the scene shifted back. The rest of the screens went dark. "Okay, what did you see?"

"It didn't strike me at first. But the videos show her going to the market."

"And?" she asked.

"She had groceries delivered a couple of times a week. The delivery guy delivered any time she wanted. So, if she's getting groceries delivered, why does she need to go to the market?"

"Good point."

"So, did she go often?"

"Collins flipped through a sheaf of pages. Yeah, you're right. For the time she was surveilled, she went twice a week. Monday and Thursday, and always around noon. Nice catch."

"Did the store have cameras? Maybe we can see if she's up to something."

Collins flipped through more pages. "Uh, yeah. The footage is in a different file. Let me see if I can pull it up." She kept one finger on the page she'd found and used her other hand to go through the directories on the computer. "There," she said as the screens came back to life. "They've put in four cameras, so we can track her as she moves through the store."

The videos were acceptable, although not as sharp as the surveillance videos taken by the agency.

"There," he said. "She's getting a cart and heading for the produce department." They watched as she walked along, not picking up anything. She left the produce department and swung by the deli. She took a proffered free sample but again put nothing into her cart.

"So far, nothing," said Collins.

Susanna turned and headed past the endcaps on the aisles. She was out of view of the store cameras for a few seconds. She reappeared, then swung up the closest aisle, headed to the front of the store, ditched the basket, and exited.

"Looks like a bust to me," said Collins.

"Uh, wait a second. Run that back, Katy. From the time she leaves the deli counter."

Collins played with the keys, and the screen showed a disjointed, comical scene in reverse.

"What did you see?" she asked.

"Look at her hand. She has both hands on the cart handle when she goes out of view. Both hands are still there when she comes out, but it looks like she has an envelope or paper in her right hand."

"A list? Maybe," she said.

"But she didn't get anything. What would she need a list for?"

They reran the video. He was right. Out of view for two seconds, and now Susanna had something new in hand.

"There. Just as she's going out of view, someone else is coming the other way," he said.

A woman wearing a long dress and a big floppy hat crossed out of view from the left, just as Susanna crossed out of view from the right.

"Can you see her face?" asked Collins.

"No, the hat hides it. A drop?"

"Yeah. That's why we don't have any phone or e-mail trace. They did a hard copy and likely burned the paper after they were done with it. I'd love to know who that other person was."

"Well, if she went every Monday and Thursday," he said, "we could look at the footage of those days and see if we get lucky," he said.

"I like the way you think," she said with a smile. *Get lucky*. I've got three more days of store video. We can start there."

The first two days were the same. Both women would disappear at the same place and time. Like the first video, the second woman always wore something that hid her face. The third video showed Susanna going out of view, but the second woman was not in the footage. Still, she emerged, stuffing a paper, or envelope, into her purse.

"The paper was put there shortly before Susanna got there. It couldn't be too long before. Go back a little further. Maybe we can catch her."

Collins rolled the tape back. As Vince had suspected, five minutes before Susanna moved behind the shelving, the second woman, wearing a large pair of sunglasses and ball cap, walked out of view, then emerged thirty seconds later."

"So, she made the drop," said Collins.

The unknown woman then progressed up the aisle. She was carrying a basket with a few items in it.

"Probably buys a few things – for cash – to keep from arousing suspicion," said Collins.

A pair of rowdy young boys came running down the aisle, not paying attention to anyone but themselves. They ran smack into the subject, dumping the contents of her basket. She bent to pick the items up as a woman came down the aisle and spoke to her. The irritated unknown woman looked up exasperated.

"Wait! Stop!" yelled Vince, staring at the screen. "There, in the mirror."

Collins backed up the video and played it slowly forward. A mirror attached to one of the shelves caught the woman's face."

"Gotcha," said Collins.

Fifty-one

Kristi barely looked at the road on her drive back to Sandy Bay. Agent Collins – Katy – was trying to get Vince transferred more than a hundred miles away. A transfer closer to where she usually was most likely stationed. But the way Collins had asked in front of her had made her both mad and depressed. Would he go? Could she stop him? Did it matter?

She pulled into the parking lot and walked to the operations center. The mystery of the sinking boat had been solved. It looked like a drug ring might be broken. She should have been happy. Instead, she was hollow inside.

She dropped into a chair.

"What's up?" asked McPherson. "Or, maybe I should ask what's down. You look like you've just lost your best friend."

"Maybe I have," she said.

"Want to talk about it?" he asked.

"It wouldn't do any good," she said. "Anything going on here?" she asked. Maybe there would be an emergency to take her mind off things.

"Nope. Oh, this did come for you," he said, picking up an envelope. "From headquarters." He handed it to her.

"I'm sure it isn't good news," she said and broke the seal. She pulled out a note. It was unsigned, but there was no mistaking Lieutenant Commander Christianson's handwriting. It read,

I hope you're happy with your decision. I'll be returning to Sandy Bay. The betrayal of your promise will cost you dearly. And, I know you are tight with Ayala. Did he tell you about his wife and child?

Kristi was sure she was going to vomit. She ran out of the office and building, hearing McPherson calling after her.

She got into her car and left the parking lot feeling depressed and angry. Her world was falling apart. She wasn't sure if she could believe Christianson, but she was hurt and angry at the thought she'd been betrayed.

She should have told Christianson everything she knew. Serve him right. Serve them all right. Not that Christianson was her friend, but she could have helped her career. Did her career even matter anymore? It seemed like everyone was lying and cheating.

She wiped a tear from her eye and started out of the lot. She didn't even know where she was going. She knew she had to put it out of her mind. Focus on something else.

She was a half-mile down the road when she remembered what Susanna had said about using real boats. Somehow, they must have known about Bob Johnson's gambling debts. And his boat was used by the smugglers to decoy the Coast Guard. And something Margaret Johnson had said kept nagging at her. She decided to go to the Johnson's home and see if either Bob or Margaret had any insights regarding who else might know about his gambling. It would keep her mind off of everything else, and if she could get additional information, she'd like to stick it to Agent Collins. It would be nice to take the wind out of her sails.

Kristi arrived at the Johnson's and parked on the street. A silver SUV was parked in front of the open garage. She walked to the door and rang the bell. No one answered. After a minute, she tried again, with the same result. So, she knocked. She was beginning to wonder if there was something wrong. She turned to walk to the garage. She saw Margaret Johnson, wearing jeans and a baggy sweatshirt, putting bags into the back of the SUV.

"Mrs. Johnson? Hi! Kristi Swanson. I wondered if I could have a few minutes of your time."

Margaret Johnson looked up, appearing startled.

"I'm sorry. I didn't mean to frighten you. I rang and knocked and didn't get an answer. I was starting to think something was wrong. Are you okay?" asked Kristi.

"Uh, yes. Yes, I'm okay. I'm just in kind of a hurry."

"Oh. Sorry. I just need a couple of minutes of your time," said Kristi.

"Well, if you'll make it quick."

"Are you going out of town?" Kristi asked as she approached the SUV and spotted suitcases in the back.

"Yes. Well, no. I'm leaving Bob. He's started gambling again. Behind my back. I want to be out of here before he gets home."

"I'm sorry to hear that. I had hoped," she said. *I know how people you trust can betray and hurt you*, she thought.

"Yeah, well, a leopard never changes its spots. I've got a couple of minutes. We can talk while I pack."

"Thank you. We've learned that the person responsible for you going out in the Francine on that stormy night was a woman named Susanna Stone. Her husband Craig was probably involved, as well. Have you ever heard of either of these people?"

Margaret Johnson looked at her, then squinted. "No. I can't say I know either of them. Do they run a gambling ring, take bets, anything like that?"

"No. They are significant drug importers and suppliers. Illegal drugs. They brought the drugs in from Mexico using boats and used the Francine as a decoy to keep the Coast Guard busy looking for a sinking vessel so they could slip their drugs past the authorities."

"I don't know any of Robert's gambling associates," said Margaret. "I can't imagine they would also be smuggling drugs, too. Unless they were, you know, gangsters."

"The thing is, I can't figure out how a big-time drug dealer would know about a relatively insignificant gambler. Much less why they would cancel his debt."

273

"It's beyond me, as well," said Margaret, "and to tell you the truth, I don't care. I've decided this part of my life is over. I'm going somewhere to start over."

"Where? Do you know?"

"I'm not sure yet. Maybe up the coast."

Kristi followed Margaret into the house and into the dining room. The table was set for dinner.

"What about your daughter?" asked Kristi.

"I'm going to pick her up at school. Then, we'll head out." There was no remorse in her voice.

"You've packed up her things as well, then?"

"Of course," said Margaret, picking up two small bags and heading for the garage.

"I'll get this," said Kristi, picking up a little girl's backpack. As she did, the backpack opened. Stacks of money were inside.

Fifty-two

Kristi turned to see Margaret Johnson pulling a small revolver from under her sweatshirt. "Ya know, I should have closed that and put it into the SUV first. But then, I didn't expect a nosy girl from the Coast Guard to show up and start asking questions."

"I don't understand," said Kristi.

"Too late to play stupid, honey. You saw the money. You'd figure it out sooner or later. If you haven't already." Margaret motioned with the gun. "Over to the chair."

Kristi hesitated.

"Look. I've got two choices here. I need time to get away. I either have to tie you up and get a day's head start or kill you now. I haven't had to kill anyone yet. Difference between jail time and a needle in the arm if they catch you, but don't think I won't if I need to. So. Over to the chair."

Kristi moved to a dining room chair on leaden legs and turned it away from the table. Every part of her body was shaking. "So, you were in on it?" She wasn't sure what 'it' entailed. She sat.

Margaret tossed her a roll of duct tape. "Do your legs around the chair legs."

"You know, you don't have to do this," said Kristi.

"Yeah, I know. I could just shoot you and get it over with." Margaret pointed the gun at her. "Keep you from testifying later. They'd probably figure it out when they found your body here." Then, quietly to herself, "Can't take time to dump her, can I?"

Kristi shivered and started to tape her left leg to the chair. There was a sound in the other room. Margaret edged toward the door, pointing the gun at Kristi and looking back and forth between her and the other room. Kristi looked behind her. Steak knives were part of the table setting. Her heart was pounding, and she felt weak. If Margaret saw or figured out what she was planning, she'd shoot her.

When Margaret turned to look into the other room, Kristi grabbed a steak knife and slid it up her right sleeve.

"Damn!" yelled Margaret.

Kristi jumped. The knife started to slide out of her sleeve. She pushed it back.

Margaret turned to her. "That cat will be the death of me yet." Then, "You're taking your time. I haven't got all day. Quick."

Kristi managed to finish her legs.

"Now, do your right arm."

Kristi complied, trying to make it look like she was doing a good job while leaving herself wiggle room. When she'd finished, Margaret took the tape and fastened her remaining limb. She stepped back from the chair and started to rip off a piece of tape.

"Don't want you getting too vocal. Getting the neighbors all involved."

"Before you do that, I'm curious. What part did you play in all this? Were you working for the Stones? I want to know. You'll probably disappear. You don't owe me, but," said Kristi.

"You're right. I don't owe you. But, what the hell. Work for the Stones? They worked for me. She knew what she was doing, but he was a complete dud. He was the frontman, and he was supposed to take the fall. Luckily, he knows nothing about my involvement. She does, but it's in her best interests not to say anything."

"Her best interests?"

"Yeah. Even if she does jail time, and she will, I have the number to a Swiss bank account. She gets the number when she's released if she doesn't rat me out. Of course, now there's you. Now I really have to run. And hide. Someplace where there's no extradition."

"But your boat. Somebody bought the gambling debt."

"I bought the debt. Idiot husband. I always hated that boat. He spent every spare minute he had on it. His baby, he called it. So, I decided to solve two problems at once. I needed a decoy to slip a large shipment through and got to punish Bob in the best way possible."

"But you were on the boat. You could have been killed."

"Yeah. I decided to go out because I figured if I didn't, he'd find some way to say it was too rough, and he had to put into a sheltered cove. So, I demanded that he take the family when he went out. I even slipped in something about Amber's dress so he'd think they were watching us. He was supposed to let enough water in to make it appear the boat was sinking, then close the valve. He let too much in and couldn't get to the valve to shut it back off. Typical. Anyway, I do appreciate that you saved us. Try not to do anything stupid. I'd rather not shoot you. My way of saying thanks." She stuffed the gun back under her sweatshirt. "Need to finish packing, and then it's adios." She put the tape over Kristi's mouth and left the dining room.

Kristi started pulling at her legs, twisting and turning. Her phone started to buzz in her pocket. There was no way she could get to it. The tape on her right leg broke first. She was also twisting her right arm as hard as she could. She heard wood splintering, and the thin arm of the dining room chair gave way. Margaret came back into the dining room. Kristi moved her right arm, trying to hide the broken chair arm.

"Still comfy?" said Margaret, giving her a cursory look. "Quick trip to the loo, and then it's goodbye." She headed out of the room.

Kristi moved her right arm with the piece of chair attached to her left arm. She stuck her fingers into her sleeve, hunting for the steak knife. Precious seconds passed. There! She pulled it out with her left hand and moved it to her right. She started slicing the duct tape, but it seemed to take forever. She freed her left hand, then moved to her legs. As she freed her left leg, she heard the toilet flushing. It took five seconds to free her right leg.

She freed herself but still had the arm of the chair taped to her. She thought about jumping Margaret when she entered the room, but Margaret had the gun. And if Margaret was faster – only one smart thing to do – escape. Escape and raise the alarm. She ran from the dining room, through the kitchen, and into the garage. Her heart was pounding. As she left the garage, she heard Margaret's voice, "You shouldn't have done that!"

Kristi ran out of the garage and to her car. She ran to the far side and ducked down. She used the steak knife to remove the piece of dining room chair still taped to her right arm, then raised her head ever so slightly and used one eye to peek around the center post. She saw Margaret standing in the garage, looking around, gun in hand. The sun was behind Kristi and in Margaret's eyes. Margaret looked out into the yard and at Kristi's car. Kristi's heart was in her throat, pounding. If Margaret saw her, she was dead. Margaret looked around. A car was coming down the street, so she stuck the gun under her sweatshirt and disappeared into the house.

Kristi opened the car door and slid into the driver's seat. She started her car. She looked down the road to safety, then looked at the SUV. "*Oh, god,*" she thought. "*I can't let her get away. Please don't let me die.*" She put the car into gear and floored the accelerator. Her car sped forward, bounced over the curb, across the lawn, and slammed into the front left corner of the SUV.

Fifty-three

Kristi tried to open her eyes, but the effort was too much. She wanted to sleep. There was shouting. Then, she was being pulled. Something hurt. She was being carried. She thought she heard a name, and then she was gone.

She slowly opened her eyes. She was in a room. White. She was lying down. She tried to move. Ow! Pain.

"Hey. Take it easy." It was Vince, standing over the bed. "The doctors want to check to make sure you didn't break anything."

"What? Where am I?"

"General Hospital. You were in a car wreck. Do you remember?" he asked.

"Oh, yeah. Margaret. Margaret Johnson. You've got to stop her! She's one of the drug smugglers."

"Yes. We know."

"You know?"

"Yes. We were going through the surveillance tapes. There were some from the market Susanna went to two days a week. We figured that was strange because she always had her groceries delivered. And that delivery boy would have hand-carried anything she wanted, so it didn't seem logical for her to go to the market twice a week. And, it was always the same times on the same days. That's where she and Margaret Johnson met. And handed off notes to each other. Margaret was handing Susanna the notes. She was careful, but I caught a glimpse of her on one of the tapes. That's how we knew she was involved. I tried to call you, but you didn't answer."

"I thought maybe she had information about who might have taken care of her husband's gambling debt," said Kristi. "I should have waited, but I realized what bothered me about our interview with her. She said she didn't know anything about boats, but she remembered the course as two eight zero. Her husband just pointed at the compass. Even if she'd noticed, she'd say the course was two hundred and eighty. Maybe just twenty-eight. And, she knew about the auto bailers not working when the boat wasn't moving. I should have known sooner that it wasn't right. She was packing. She said she was leaving her husband because he'd started gambling again. I picked up the daughter's backpack, and it was full of money. That's when she pulled a gun and tied me up." She looked away. "I wanted to one-up Agent Collins. Maybe impress you."

"Impress me. Why? You're smart, strong, beautiful, and someone who makes me feel special."

"Shouldn't you be saying this to your wife?" she asked, turning away from him. Her tone was cold.

"Who told you I had a wife?" he asked.

"That's not important. I just happened to find out you not only have a wife but a child, too." She turned back to confront him, wincing in pain as she did. "Were you trying to keep it a secret? Well, it's a hell of a secret. You've kept it from me for years! Where are they? They aren't anywhere near Sandy Bay, that's for sure. Do you even send them money?"

"You want to hear the story?" he asked.

He didn't seem to be contrite. She was determined to be tough. "Fine. This better be good," she said, trying to mimic the tone Dee had used with Agent Way on the San Lorenzo.

"Yeah. I was married. Was. A long time ago. Just after I'd gotten into the service, I met her at a picnic. We started to date. She seemed interested in me. Listened to me. Things were pretty good physically, as well. We got married."

Kristi didn't change her expression.

"I was working hard. Day and night. I wanted to make good." He paused. "That's when I met Scott. I started doing drug interdiction. The first time out, I almost got my head shot off. If Scott hadn't been there," he said, letting it die. "I've learned to keep my head down."

"Anyway, after we married and I started working harder, she didn't seem interested in bedroom calisthenics. She spent a lot of time at the gym. I was tired from the job, so I didn't mind. I'd hoped we'd find time together later. After I'd earned some rank."

283

He opened a thermos, poured some coffee, and offered her some. She shook her head.

"About a year after we were married, maybe a few months more, she decided she wanted to have a baby. She became pretty aggressive sexually. It didn't matter how tired I was. It wasn't long before she announced she was pregnant, but she continued going to the gym regularly. She gave birth to a baby boy eight months later. The doctor said all the exercise may have contributed to the premature birth."

He took another sip of his coffee.

"I was going through the hospital records one day, a couple of months later, and discovered his blood type was AB positive. I figured there had to be a mistake because my wife and I were A positive. I found a way to have all of us retested without causing suspicion, and there was no change."

"Oh no!" said Kristi, breaking her expression.

"Yeah. When I confronted her, first she said there must be a mistake. When that didn't work, she said they must have switched babies. That one didn't pass the laugh test, either. Pressed, she finally told me she'd gone to a party with a friend and passed out drunk. She had no idea someone had taken advantage of her. She was embarrassed and didn't want to tell me. She claimed to want a baby, so I'd have sex with her, and she could cover."

"That's terrible! How could she," started Kristi.

"Finally, I contacted her friend, and I found out she'd had multiple affairs with guys at the gym."

"Oh my god!" said Kristi. "What did you do?"

"I got myself a lawyer. A good one. Cheap. The guy who'd gotten my wife – correction – ex-wife pregnant was married to a divorce attorney. She castrated him in the legal sense. Pro bono. The former Mrs. Ayala and not-my-son headed off to parts unknown. I haven't seen or heard from them in more than a dozen years."

She sighed and put her hand on his arm. "I'm sorry. I shouldn't have doubted you."

"Who gave you this little tidbit, by the way?"

"Lieutenant Commander Christianson. She sent a note to Sandy Bay. Just after I heard Agent Collins essentially proposition you."

"I'm not interested in Agent Collins. Or the San Diego office. I'm happy right where I am."

"Yeah, but Collins is all that and makes more money. And, I think she wants you," she said.

"Well, she can't have me. I'm working on a better deal. And if money were all that important, I'd be working my tail off for that next promotion."

Kristi turned back and looked at him. A smile crossed her face. "So, how did I end up here?"

"When we identified Margaret Johnson as Susanna Craig's contact, we went to arrest her. I called you to let you know. We jumped into Katy's car and used the flashers to get there as fast as possible. We saw Margaret next to your car, crashed into hers. She had a gun in her hand and a backpack. The backpack you saw. It was full of money. A little over a hundred thousand."

"When she saw us, she pointed her gun at us. Katy jumped out of the car and pulled hers. Margaret Johnson decided not to start a gunfight and dropped her gun. We called 911, and the rest you can probably figure out. What you did was incredibly brave but incredibly stupid. What were you thinking?"

"Katy, huh?"

"That's what you got from that entire explanation?"

Kristi stared at him.

"Fine. She wanted me to call her Katy. Don't assume anything more."

"I thought about just driving away, but she said she had money hidden overseas. Swiss accounts. At the last second, I decided that I didn't want her to get away, and the only way to stop her was to make it so she couldn't drive the SUV. It was the only thing I could think of. When can I get out of here?" she asked.

"When the doctors clear you. They want to make sure you aren't injured. Another day, probably. It would have been better if you'd fastened your seat belt. Thank God for airbags. Otherwise, it would have been a lot worse."

"My car! What about my car?" she asked.

"Totaled, I'm afraid."

"Damn! I don't suppose insurance," she started to ask.

"Well, actually, the insurance company's first response was that this was an intentional self-inflicted accident, that is, you meant to crash your car. As such, it won't be covered."

"Oh, God! Now, what do I do?"

"We'll figure out something. I'll pick you up and drop you off for the time being."

"But I just paid it off! I was looking forward to having some extra money. Now, I will have to find another car and start paying a loan all over."

"As I said, we'll think of something. You stopped the bad guy," he said.

"And look what it cost me. This day has gone from bad to worse. What else can possibly go wrong?"

"Um, well, I hate to be the bearer of bad news, but Commander Christianson has been cleared of any intentional wrong-doing and has returned as the OIC of Sandy Bay."

"That was in the note she sent me. I won't ask what else."

"Maybe she will have mellowed a bit," he said.

287

"Not from what I read in her note. She wants blood." Kristi paused, looked heavenward, then looked at him. "I have something to confess."

He looked at her. "I can't imagine it could be too bad, knowing you."

"It's bad enough. The reason I followed you the night you went out on the Bayliner and the night I followed you to the marina wasn't because I was worried or curious. Lieutenant Commander Christianson told me that if I wanted her endorsement on my commission program application, I'd have to find out what you were doing when you were called away and tell her."

"And did you?" he asked.

"I was going to, but after you caught me and the XO told me not to say anything, I was caught between doing what I thought was right and doing what she wanted so I could go for a commission. I'm sorry. I should have told you."

"But in the end, you did what was right."

"Don't think I didn't have moments where I wasn't sure what I would do," she said. "Now, she knows that I knew and didn't tell her. She'll be out to make life miserable. And I'll never get that endorsement. Can you forgive me?"

"There's nothing to forgive. And, I wouldn't worry about her. I'm still a buffer between the two of you. She'll be hard-pressed to find anything."

"Thank you. By the way, how long have I been here?"

288

"About ten hours."

"And you've been here all that time?" she asked.

"Yes, all that time. And, yes, I was worried. Please don't do anything like that again. I want you around a while."

"Well, maybe you should take care of me," she said with a smile, "just to make sure." She was still smiling as she closed her eyes.

Fifty-four

Lieutenant Commander Christianson had been reinstated for a week. Kristi had avoided seeing her personally. Then, she was ordered to report to Captain Yarrow's office at nine in the morning.

Kristi entered the Executive Officer's office and stood at attention in front of his desk. She hadn't eaten, and she was glad she hadn't. Anything in her stomach might have landed on the XO's desk. Vince was standing in the corner. Lieutenant Commander Christianson sat in a chair placed to the side.

"Petty Officer Kristi Swanson reporting as ordered, sir." She waited for the command to stand at ease.

"Do you know why I've asked you to come here, Petty Officer Swanson?"

"Uh, not exactly, sir." There was no command to 'stand at ease.'

Captain Yarrow picked up a folder from his desk and opened it. "Lieutenant Commander Christianson has come to me with some allegations. I thought it best to look into them informally rather than in an official venue."

Kristi's knees started to go weak. There were sparkles in her vision.

Captain Yarrow closed the folder and placed it on his desk. "The first of these allegations has to do with the violation of regulations and standard operating procedures on April 28, when you took a small craft out alone during a storm and failed to return when your fuel reached the critical level. Can you enlighten me?" He was impassive.

Kristi's face was hot, and she knew, red. "Sir, we had a distress call. There were only three of us on duty that evening. Chief Ayala was on special assignment at headquarters."

Yarrow looked at Vince.

"Yes, sir. I'd gotten a call to report to headquarters for the evening."

Yarrow looked at Kristi. "Continue."

"Well, Petty Officer McPherson, our medical technician, made a run to the hospital for supplies. It would have taken almost an hour to go out if I were to wait for him to return. Petty Officer Pritchett, the third person on duty, had to stay at the station. That left me. My choice was between waiting an hour or going out by myself. The distress call sounded urgent. I was the senior NCO at the station, and I made the decision to go. When I reached the Francine, she had maybe ten or fifteen minutes before she sank."

"Chief?" said Yarrow looking at Vince.

"Yes, sir, that is correct. There were no other rescue vessels in the area. If Petty Officer Swanson had not acted as she had, the three people on that boat would have drowned. And there was an article in the local paper about the rescue, praising the station's effort, and Commander Christianson in particular," he said, nodding in the direction of the OIC.

Yarrow looked at Lieutenant Commander Christianson. "I can explain, sir," she said. "I had nothing to do with." Yarrow silenced her by raising his hand.

Yarrow looked at Kristi. "And your fuel?"

"I calculated how much I had and planned to turn around within the next five minutes when I spotted the sinking boat. It took a few minutes to get the passengers on board. I ran at best fuel use speed. Yes, by the time I returned, the tank was practically dry. But even if I had run out of fuel, I still think it would have been better than having three people drown."

Yarrow sat quietly for two minutes. It seemed like forever to Kristi.

"The second issue has to do with a line of duty investigation requested by Commander Christianson," Yarrow continued, "regarding the automobile accident in which you were involved and your subsequent hospitalization. She states the accident was intentional and therefore is not in the line of duty. If true, it would be an unauthorized absence for the time you were out."

"Sir," said Vince, "Petty Officer Swanson was threatened by a drug dealer and held against her will. She escaped and could have left the scene but used her vehicle to disable the perpetrator's to prevent her from leaving. Agent Collins arrested that person on the scene. She had significant assets and might have evaded law enforcement if she had gotten away. I have a statement from FBI Agent Katy Collins stating that Petty Officer Swanson's help was invaluable in the arrest."

He didn't say anything about me not being authorized to go to the Johnson's and how I placed myself in the situation, she thought.

Yarrow paused. "Thank you, Chief Ayala. There is one other thing, and this concerns you, as well, chief." He opened the folder and pulled out a photograph. "Commander Christianson has given me this photograph. It shows you and Petty Officer Swanson coming out of her apartment. Commander Christianson stated she believes it is proof of fraternization."

Kristi's stomach was turning over. Did they know about the weekend she spent with Vince? He wasn't really, well technically, her superior then. Did it matter?

"May I see the photograph?" asked Vince.

Yarrow handed it to him.

"When was this taken?" he asked.

Yarrow looked and Commander Christianson.

"That shouldn't matter," she snapped.

"The date, commander," said Yarrow.

"I'm – I'm not sure," she answered.

"Then it must be someone else who took this," said Yarrow. "Who gave it to you?"

"It was placed under my office door. I don't know who," she lied.

"When?" asked Yarrow.

"I don't remember. Exactly. The second half of May. On a Monday. Maybe the twenty-second."

"Chief?" asked Yarrow.

Ayala thought for a minute. "Sir, that would seem to be a day after Petty Officer Swanson and I were at headquarters. We'd worked through the night and were in meetings with yourself and agents Collins and Way that morning. I had to take Petty Officer Swanson to pick up her car. She asked to stop at her apartment first. For a change of clothing."

"Oh, yes," said Yarrow. "I recall. That was about the same time if Commander Christianson's recollection is accurate." Yarrow leaned back in his chair. He stared at the ceiling and interlaced his fingers, and placed his hands behind his head. At length, he sat up straight.

"I don't see any substance in any of these allegations, Commander," he said, looking at her. "As far as the first one goes, you personally would seem to have benefitted from Petty Officer Swanson's bravery without having taken any part in the action yourself. And as far as her accident, it may have been a bit rash, but again, I commend her for assisting in the apprehension of a dangerous drug dealer and putting her life at risk."

He replaced the photograph in the folder and closed it. "Finally, the photograph in question would seem to have been taken the morning after Chief Ayala and Petty Officer Swanson had completed an overnight work assignment. Chief Ayala was taking Miss Swanson to retrieve her vehicle, and it doesn't seem inappropriate that they stopped for her to change before continuing."

Christianson's face was scarlet.

"What does bother me," he continued, "is that you have called into question acts of heroism by Petty Officer Swanson that warrant awards, not reprimands. You would seem to have benefitted personally from one of them. And while I'm happy that you were cleared of any intentional involvement in aiding drug smuggling activities, I would suggest that it would be best not to draw undue attention to these things in light of your perceived involvement. Do I make myself clear?" he asked.

"Yes, sir."

"You are all dismissed," he said. "Oh, chief, would you mind staying for a minute?"

Kristi followed Commander Christianson out of the office and closed the door. When they were in the hallway alone, Christianson turned toward her, her face twisted with anger.

"This isn't over, missy. You'll never get that endorsement even if hell freezes over. I'll pull in every favor I have left." She turned and stomped off.

The XO's door opened, and Vince appeared. "You okay?" he asked. "You look like you've seen a ghost."

"The ghost of my career. Commander Christianson just said she was going to get me. Call in all the favors she has left to do it. This day is going from bad to worse." She paused. "What did the XO want?"

"He wanted to know how the station was doing. And how you are doing after the accident. How thin we're stretched. He wants to add to your responsibilities."

"I don't know. I feel kind of drained. What does he want to add?" she asked.

"Well, you've now got a top-secret clearance, and he'd like to have your help with drug interdiction. You'll be working out of headquarters. Not out of Sandy Bay. Light duty for a while so you can recover completely."

She looked at him. "Then, I won't see you." Her being deflated.

"Well, not during the day, anyway," he said smiling.

Fifty-five

Kristi and Annie sat in the shade outside of the headquarters cafeteria. They each had a salad.

"So, how's it going here at HQ?" asked Annie.

"Okay," responded Kristi. "I miss being at Sandy Bay. The work was more fun. People were my friends. It's a lot more impersonal here. I guess what Vince said was right. Now I know for sure why he prefers the small stations." She stuck a forkful of salad into her mouth.

"Yeah, more of a homey atmosphere – if you can overlook the venom coming from the OIC."

"Is it that bad?" asked Kristi.

"It's pretty bad. Her good friend Lieutenant Bond broke down during his court-martial and was released from the service with an other-than-honorable discharge. All he gets is mental health services. And, she's been put on notice that when her contract is up, she won't be eligible for an extension. So, she's out."

"Wow! What is she going to do?" asked Kristi.

"She's applying for some low-level management positions. If she gets one, they may let her go early. Can you imagine being in a company and reporting to her?"

"No. But, how do you know?"

"She told me to type up her resume and the applications. I held them for a day to take a look, then told her that I couldn't do her personal work because it wasn't government business. I thought the top of her head was going to come off."

"You'll be lucky if she doesn't find some way to hurt you."

"She doesn't have a chance. Any input she has goes through the XO, and Captain Yarrow and I go back. Besides, she's busy with other things."

"What other things?" asked Kristi.

"Well, there was a leak in the plumbing. Flooded out her office."

"Oh no! Did they find the source?"

"Um, yeah. They had to dig up her reserved parking spot to get to it. They got the leak fixed, but it'll be about a month before the spot can be repaved."

"This sounds suspicious."

"Well, stuff happens. Karma, and all that."

Kristi laughed. "I have an idea it was more than just coincidence the leak screwed up her office and her parking spot. If I didn't know better, I'd think a certain chief petty officer had something to do with it."

"I have no idea what you mean."

"How are you doing there, Annie?"

"It's quiet. So far, there isn't anyone I can confide in. Vince stops in daily. That helps, but there's only so much I can talk about with him. Christianson tried to throw her weight around for a while, but I've ignored her. I'm hoping they transfer someone like you in. Or another OIC like Dee. That'd be nice."

Two men approached. Kristi recognized the commanding officer, Captain Lyle Goodman. He was with a tall, athletic-looking man wearing a well-tailored dark blue suit, white shirt, and bow tie. She guessed him to be in his fifties

Kristi came to attention. "Good afternoon, captain."

Annie ran to the man in the suit. "Uncle Claude! How great to see you!" She put her arms around him and hugged him.

He hugged her in return. "And how is my favorite niece?"

"Just great. Better now that you're here. Oh, this is Kristi Swanson, my good friend and the woman I told you about."

The commanding officer started to speak, but the other man cut him off.

"Well, Petty Officer Swanson, it is a pleasure to meet you. I've heard all kinds of almost unbelievable things about you. Well, except that they came from Annie."

"Thank you, sir. I'm not sure what Annie has told you. I've just tried to do my job."

"Nonsense. I understand you risked your life not once but twice to save others and apprehend a dangerous criminal."

"Actually, sir, the FBI apprehended the criminal. I played a minor part in delaying her until the arresting officer arrived," said Kristi.

"All that, and modesty, as well. I understand you lost your car in this delaying action."

"Um, yes, sir. I still have to replace it."

"Well, I think there's a way we can help with that." He turned to the commanding officer. "So, I would hope that there is an award in the works for this young woman, Lyle."

Lyle? Kristi thought. *Who calls the commanding officer by his first name?*

"Yes, Senator. There is one in the works. One was started earlier but got held up somehow."

"Well, make sure it is appropriate, not just a merit badge. She deserves something that shows respect for her actions." He turned to Kristi. "It has been an honor to meet you. I'd like to be here when you receive your award." He turned to the commanding officer, "That shouldn't be a problem, should it, Lyle?"

"No, Senator. I'll be sure to coordinate with your office."

"Just let Annie know. I can fly out for the weekend. Get some quality time with her." He turned to Annie. "Let's have dinner tonight. I don't know many places here. Let me know the time and place. I'll pick you up." Then, "Why don't you have Kristi join us, as well."

He hugged Annie, shook Kristi's hand, and then walked away with the commanding officer. As he walked away, Kristi heard the Senator say, "Lyle, as the chair of the Senate Commerce, Science, and Transportation Committee, I want to assure you that we're not going to be asking for base closures. We're working with the House to ensure your budget grows, not shrinks."

"Senator?!" said Kristi, turning toward Annie.

"Oh, didn't I mention my uncle is a Senator? Senator Claude Hudson. Where do you want to go for dinner tonight?"

They were interrupted again by the approach of Agent Way.

"Hi," she said. "I, uh, congratulations on helping to get Margaret Johnson. Took courage. I apologize for some of the things I said. You were a real value in this investigation."

"No problem. What can I do for you?" asked Kristi.

"Um, more what I can do for you." She opened a folder and produced photographs of three cars, a Honda SUV, a Ford Mustang, and a Chevy Malibu. "See anything you like?" she asked.

"I see everything I like. What's the deal?" asked Kristi.

"We seize cars from drug dealers. Every so often, we hold an auction to get rid of them. I'm about to hold a small auction.

We'll start the bidding at one dollar. If there are no other bids, the car is yours."

Kristi studied the photos, "I don't," she started.

"The Mustang was run pretty hard. The others belonged to a wife who never drove them. Low mileage."

"So, I guess the smart money would be the SUV or Malibu."

"So, you want to start the bidding at one dollar?" asked Way.

"Uh, yeah, sure. One dollar for the Honda SUV." She giggled.

"Are there any other bids?"

Annie remained silent.

"Going once. Going twice. Sold to the lady in uniform for one dollar." Way put out her hand.

Kristi dug in her pocket, pulled out a dollar, and handed it to her.

Agent Way handed her a piece of paper. "Here is the release. You can pick it up at impound at your convenience," then she turned and walked away.

"Well, I'll be," said Kristi.

Epilog

They sat slumped on either end of the couch in Vince's apartment. He sipped his drink and set the glass on the side table. Kristi's untouched wine sat on the coffee table.

"What's on your mind?" he asked.

"Nothin'," she answered.

"Can't be 'nothin.' You never let wine sit that long."

She sighed. "I wanted the commission so badly. I wanted to show my family. My friends. I wanted to be important. Self-sufficient."

"You are important."

"Yeah, well. I found out that I couldn't do what Commander Christianson wanted me to do so I could get her endorsement. I would have betrayed you. And the service."

"More importantly," he said, "you would have betrayed yourself. You couldn't do that. I'm proud of you for that."

"She told me I'd never get an endorsement. I wonder if I would have been a good officer," she said quietly.

"I think so. Yes. I know so."

"I'm not even sure if I want it anymore. I mean, look at Commander Christianson. She doesn't think about the mission or the people. All she worries about is getting promoted and sitting in a big building. Her friend Bond, giving out information so he could keep seeing Mrs. Stone," she said.

"That doesn't mean you have to be that kind of an officer. Most people in the service care about the mission and their people," he said.

"Anyway, you were right. Even if I got a commission, I'd likely be stuck in meetings that would be sucking the life out of me. Or doing some insignificant paper pushing. That's enough reason."

"Yes, that's one of the reasons I decided chief was enough. It allows me to do the things I like. And I can have my retirement without doing all that administrative stuff. I can still take a boat out. But those aren't the only reasons. Besides, you shouldn't live your life according to what I've decided might be best for me," he said.

"What other reason is there?" she asked.

"I told you about my former wife."

"Yes."

"When we were getting divorced," he started, looking at the floor, "she said something I've never forgotten. She said that she had affairs because of my ambition. I was working all the time, and I paid no attention to her." He looked at her, then said, "I neglected her. And she found other company." He sipped his drink and looked at the floor. "I've – I've always wondered if that might be true. Instead of ignoring the people around me, I decided that I'd throttle back, and if I ever met anyone, the job wouldn't kill the relationship."

"That's ridiculous," said Kristi. "She said that to make you feel bad, or herself better. She couldn't or wouldn't take responsibility for what she did, so somebody else had to be at fault. You. She likely blamed the guys she had affairs with, too. There are many successful, busy people who don't have spouses sleeping with their entire zip codes."

"Truth is," he said, "I love it the way it is. I don't go to those meetings or waste my life doing paperwork. I get to take a boat out whenever I want. I don't worry about the next selection board and whether I'll be promoted. I don't worry about whether every thing I do and every decision I make are in the best interests of my career. I'm friends with people I like. They know I'm not a threat, and I don't have to put up with others who would be trying to stab me in the back to get ahead."

Kristi just looked at him, wondering what to say. He was content in his world. How many people could say that?

"But we were talking about you," he said. "Don't rule it out. You're up for an award. And, Christianson's endorsement doesn't matter. She's gone after her current contract is up. Disgraced, even if they've said she technically did nothing wrong. You can get that commission yet. School online or off-hours. Direct commission. Decide what you want to do once you have your degree."

"Yeah. But if I get that commission, anything we might have had will be illegal. Fraternization and all."

"It doesn't have to be," he said, turning toward her. "You're at headquarters now. You don't have to worry about Christianson. And, I'm no longer your supervisor. No impediment. I've known married enlisted couples where one gets a commission, and the other doesn't. That's not against regulations." He looked at her and paused. "I've got a ring box in my coat and a question I've been dying to ask you. If you say yes, we'll be okay, no matter what happens down the line."

"In that case," she said, with a sly smile, "the wine can wait, and we can start the honeymoon right now." She rolled on top of him, pinned him down, and kissed him passionately.

About this Book

The United States Coast Guard was founded in 1790 and has a long proud history. More than one hundred coastguardsmen were killed in action during the 1944 D-Day invasion of Europe. Coastguardsmen have also served in action in other conflicts as well – riding small boats on the rivers of Viet Nam and riverine operations in Iraq, for example. During peacetime, the Coast Guard performs drug interdiction, stops human trafficking, and provides security of our ports and shores against those wishing to do us harm – along with about a dozen other missions vital to our nation. During 2015, the Coast Guard saved over 3,500 lives during rescues. That year they also saved more than 33,500 lives during Hurricane Katrina.

This is a book of fiction. Any similarity to any persons or events is coincidental. Fraternization between active-duty supervisory personnel and those they supervise is punishable under the Uniform Code of Military Justice (UCMJ), although fraternization does occur from time to time, despite the prohibition. Love, in real life as in fiction, sometimes does conquer all.

Coast Guard officers and enlisted personnel perform their duties with honor and distinction. When you see them, please thank them for their service. They go to war against a vast array of miscreants and enemies on a daily basis.

The decompression times used for the two-hundred-foot dive in chapter forty-six were estimated. Dives to that depth should only be undertaken by divers trained for deep diving. Solo diving is never recommended for sport divers.

Thank you for reading my book! I hope you enjoyed it.

If you liked this book, please leave a review on Amazon. Reviews help other readers find books they would like to read and help authors improve their own works.

In addition, if you would like to be someone who reads my books before publication and who receives the completed book free of charge, please send your name and e-mail address to my publisher at TWeaver2008@aol.com to be included in this group. You may opt out at any time. You can also contact me through my website https://www.annaleighromance.com/

Books by Anna Leigh

Valerie – A Love Story (paperback only)

Loves Lost and Found – A Mystery Romance Adventure

Lost in the Forest – A Romantic Wilderness Adventure

River Cruise Undercover – A Romantic Travel Adventure

Rocky Mountain Romance

Shallow Water Romance – A Story of Forbidden Love and Adventure

Secrets of the Deep – A Romantic Adventure

Shallow Water Intrigue – A Story of Romance and Mystery

ABOUT THE AUTHOR

Anna Leigh lives in suburban Maryland. She enjoys musical theater, loves to travel, and cares for small animals. She also enjoys fitness activities, has completed numerous Spartan challenges, and placed in her class in the Strongest Woman Maryland competition.

www.ingramcontent.com/pod-product-compliance
Lightning Source LLC
Chambersburg PA
CBHW031247170626
46807CB00001B/30